ALSO BY MAX APPLE

The Oranging of America

Max Apple

A Novel
of the Left
and the Right

The Viking Press

New York

Copyright © Max Apple, 1978

First published in 1978 by The Viking Press
625 Madison Avenue, New York, N.Y. 10022

Published simultaneously in Canada by
Penguin Books Canada Limited

LIBRARY OF CONGRESS CATALOGING IN PUBLICATION DATA
Apple, Max.
Zip : a novel of the left and the right.
I. Title.
pz4.a6476zi   [ps3551.p56]   813'.5'4   77–28363
isbn 0–670–79692–1

Printed in the United States of America
Set in Linotype Fairfield.

I would like to express my gratitude to the National Endow-
ment for the Arts for the grant which made it possible for me to
finish this work.

Zip is a work of fiction and its content derives entirely from my
imagination. Where I have used real names or what seem to be
physical descriptions of real people, it is done purely in the interest
of fiction. In any serious sense the similarities between the char-
acters in this novel and the real lives of any persons living or dead
are unintended and coincidental.

—Max Apple

For Bashy and for Rachmiel

ZIP

1

Let me steal nothing more from you, Jesús, my middle-weight. The story is all yours, conqueror of the roped-off ring, hero of the dusty Third World streets. In history you will stand as an image of the possible, a breaker of boundaries. But when I first saw you, all I could offer was $1.65 per hour as a breaker of batteries.

Even in your desperation you shined. Nearly asleep on the porch of our tiny office, jacketless in the ice cold Michigan November, you arose to let me enter. In the midst of your shivering, even there, I could see your dignity.

"Señor," you said, "I am an innocent man waylaid by circumstance."

Circumstance Ira Goldstein understands, innocence too. I give you my extra jacket, a dollar advance for breakfast, and then your own fifteen-pound sledge-hammer to beat the lead free of battery casing, the precious lead that keeps Momma and me in business. Momma thinks I'm crazy to hire someone whom I find sleeping outside the office door.

"This is no romantic story about orphans," she says. "This is the real world. In the real world you're the orphan and I'm the widow. And this is a junkyard, not a charity for drunken Mexicans."

Jesús listens to it all. His body is tense. His young cheeks have no hint of beard. You can see at once that

1

he has learned to roll with insults. He hands me my jacket. "Jesús will go. Thanks, buddy," he says.

"Wait," I say, "my mother talks like this all the time. She has become hardened by the business world because of tough breaks. Give her a few weeks and she'll be bringing you homemade sponge cake."

Frieda laughs. "All right," she says, "lead is forty-six cents a pound with this Mexican and forty-six cents without him. Maybe with a little help you'll get out more too."

Momma's desire for me to get out, her never-ending passion to do right for her only child, enters into each of her decisions. You, Jesús, a waif on the doorstep, you have no obligations. Earn a living, stay out of jail, register to vote—for you this is plenty. But for me the business of daily life has to lead to a direct dividend. Two hundred dollars a week, a reasonably good house, a color TV, a one-year-old pickup, a good credit rating, all this is not enough. Grandma needs offspring. The pressure is on my loins to produce. But before those loins even have a chance, the mouth has to make small talk, the eyes have to look straight at the girls who terrify me, the hands have to make promising gestures. In one of the books that she carried with her from Lithuania Grandma shows me significant passages that guarantee eternal life to those who live long enough to witness a great-grandchild. It is 1966, and Grandma is no superstitious fool. She knows the odds are long, but she trusts the wisdom of the past. Also, to encourage me can do no harm. "Get some zip," she says. "Go out, get married."

She and Frieda don't want me to be trapped by the burden of themselves. They would gladly live alone in poverty if necessary just so their twenty-four-year-old Ira could find a nice girl and live as bland a life as any salesman in Detroit.

2

Five days a week I man the scale, and roam the yard full of battery carcasses and rusted radiators. But to Momma and Grandma I am a prince among these ruins. They don't understand why the girls of Detroit are not marching in groups around our house to demand that I go out more. Grandma thinks I should begin to telephone fathers to ask their permission; Momma wants me to attend more mixers at the community center.

While they plan my future, you, Jesús, a stranger, you save my life. When I am in the greatest peril, I see for the first time your speed and power. From the perch of my own fear I learn to trust you. It's three below zero in the office. Moses Robinson has me backed against the wall. "Who says a ton is two thousand pounds? If it was two thousand pounds they'd call it two tons." He wants to be paid on the basis of a 1000-pound ton. He is wild, irrational, mean. He weighs at least 240. Frieda screams, "Give him whatever he wants, he'll kill you!" And it looks as if he might.

"Pay, Jewman," he says, "or you'll be brushin' your teeth through your ass." I see the gold rims of his teeth, the pores of his black skin. I am too paralyzed to move, but my mother is beside me handing him money.

"I want the Jewman to give it to me. I want a receipt." He is smiling an ugly, triumphant smile. Then Jesús steps into the tiny office.

"Señor," he says to Moses Robinson, "leave this man alone. He is telling you the truth. A ton is two thousand pounds."

"Mind your own fucking business," Robinson says, "or I'll wipe the shit off the walls with you too."

Jesús smiles. He is ready. "Try it," he says. Robinson turns toward Jesús.

Frieda pulls me to the door. She wants me to run to the truck and go for help. "Wait," I say. "I don't want to leave Jesús here alone. Robinson was a fighter. He went

3

ten rounds with Ezzard Charles." My father took me to see that fight. When I first met Moses Robinson I idolized him. Now he is a hulk, aging but powerful, moving in on young Jesús.

Of course Robinson throws the first punch, and of course Jesús destroys him with clean and effortless punches like a television policeman. Jesús spreads Robinson across the floor. The black man is more embarrassed than hurt. I write his receipt for a thousand pounds and hand him his cash. He departs in silence.

"Thank you," Frieda says. "You have saved Ira from a beating, maybe death. We can never thank you enough."

And what way, Jesús, did I find to thank you—the way of exploitation and greed. The way of setting every man against every other man. I know what you have written about those years. I agree. My penitence is complete and yet do you remember how innocent we both were? You were eighteen years old, Jesús, fresh from street crime, and what did I know? I read *Sport* magazine and *Ring*, and still daydreamed about playing for the Detroit Tigers. That night I imagined us in center ring, me holding your glove aloft as the TV cameras ground out our image and the roar of the crowd declared us winners forever. It was almost the first good dream I had been able to sustain in years. My father was there too: Abe, risen from the grave to be in your corner. He wore a shirt that said *Jesús*. His face was indistinct, but I recognized him from the stoop of his shoulders. He didn't say much. His resurrection was not important when we were going for the championship. This my father understood. In returning, as in life, he shunned the spotlight. It was so real that I could taste your sweat when we hugged.

"What are you going to do, Ira," Howard Cosell

asked, "now that your fighter has won the champion-ship? How are you going to top a success like that?"

"Howard," I tell him and the millions watching, "we're going to Florida. I'm getting for my mother and grandmother a small condominium in a Jewish neigh-borhood. It's good-bye forever to the scrap business. And the cold Michigan winters. They will clip coupons and eat fresh ocean fish."

"But what about you, the architect of this splendid triumph?"

"I, Howard, am going to marry Karen Cole, who sat across from me in tenth grade study hall. She used to go steady with football players, but now she has matured and recognizes my worth. Her tits point skyward. Girls envy her lift and posture. If she is watching I want to say 'Hi, Karen, I have not forgotten you.' I will watch over Jesús and develop other promising talent. Florida is a good home base for working with Latins. Of course I'll give lots of money to the United Jewish Appeal and may even let Jesús fight an exhibition in Israel. I'll do what I can for world peace as well."

"Good luck," Howard Cosell wishes me as I spread the ropes for Jesús and follow him out of the ring through the cheering mass into the wintergreen-smelling locker room.

"Where did you get the idea of starting this young Puerto Rican on the road to the championship?" Cosell asks. He has followed me to the locker room. I tell him about the Moses Robinson incident. "Naturally," he says. "You saw a super talent and you were determined to develop it to its full potential. This is one of the problems with the contemporary world. Nobody works to his potential. The black men in your scrap yard, for example, could break dozens more batteries each, and you yourself could take three night classes per semester rather than two. And the brain as we all know scarcely gets any use at all. Instead of daydreaming about naked girls you could learn a little about the stock market and tax laws. Would this kill you? And while you're at it, how about studying a little Hebrew, to give *nachas* to your grandmother. How many years does she have left? Show a little respect. Don't run out of the room when she asks you to point out the department store sales in the newspaper. Not everyone is as interested as you are in the Vietnam war. Grandma wants Hudson's and Wurzburg's to stay in business too, just like you want Hanoi. You weren't born yet in the Depression when Hudson's gave your mother a job and kept the family going on her eight dollars a week. For that you'll owe them always. On white sale days, on end-of-month clearances, Grandma wants to repay her debt to Hudson's and get a few bargains too."

"I agree," I tell him, "but it was in order to develop all the fine qualities of life that I pursued my career as a manager and gave Jesús the inspiration and financial backing that he needed."

"But your grandmother," he chides me, "she never wanted her only grandson to end up like this, in the boxing ring with half-naked brutes and gamblers and loose women of all kinds."

"Sacrifices have to be made. In this century there is little purity. My grandma lives in another world. To her a supermarket is as revolutionary as space travel. I have given up trying to modernize her."

"Does this mean," Cosell asks, "that you no longer will come home from school and translate for her some of the English classics into Yiddish? Does it mean that you will not watch TV with her as you watched *I Love Lucy* and the *$64,000 Question* in your childhood?

"And how about her bad leg. Now that you are a famous manager and an international celebrity, are you going to neglect wrapping her arthritic knee in the red flannel that she says helps her? Are you going to insist that she remove the copper bracelet that keeps her wrist from aching? Is she going to be too much of an embarrassment—this remnant of Lithuania who can't even write English?"

Jesús interrupts. "Listen, boys, Ira is tired. So am I. The fighter and manager need some rest. And we've got strategy to work on, especially while his father, Abe, is around to help us out. Did you boys know that Abe was a fight fan? Yes, much more than his son Ira. Had Abe been alive I would have been an even surer thing."

The locker room is awash in cold beer and champagne. Frieda brings in trays of cold cuts and homemade strudel. How the fight fans and reporters dig into the strudel. This everyone loves. This was the strudel that Dr. Shimmer used to snack on—Dr. Shimmer who signed Abe's death certificate, who called one night to say that Abe Goldstein had rolled a seven but life must go on. How he loved that strudel that Frieda used to give him when he visited Abe's hospital room. He held it away from his white gown so the crumbs wouldn't disturb other patients. He chewed in small, slow bites. All the time that he snacked he left the cold hard stethoscope on Abe's heart. Frieda and little Ira huddled at the side of the bed, waiting for the report on the heart. Today the heart is good, bad, so so? Always noncommittal, Dr. Shimmer merely said, "OK." He wrote notes. Not for you to peck at, little Ira. He wrote these notes for the nurses, whose high starched rumps you longed for even in those days, barely past your Bar Mitzvah. Your poor father's veins so choked by cholesterol that barely enough blood slipped through to keep his legs cold and clammy. And you, being an open pig about circulation, getting hard-ons for the nurses. If you're not careful you'll end up no better than Abe. Remember what Miss

7

Davis said, "You must be kind to your heart." Miss Davis says, "It never gets a total rest, it works all day and all night. How would you like to work as hard as your heart works?" It is a question, Miss Davis, that has stayed with me. Thanks to you, I rest my hardy little worker lest I exploit him and the heart goes on to strike me dead. "An ingrate," says the heart, "he lies, he abused me, he didn't keep his head down the way you said to, Miss Davis. He played with himself too much, making me pump all that extra blood to his groin. He ran nonstop home from school. He lived in fear of bad grades. From him I never got a moment's rest. Since third grade he has never during the day taken those twenty-five deep, slow breaths that you told him about. He has not imagined himself on a nice calm beach with the sun just so, a light breeze across his flesh and the ocean making a soothing noise in the background. He is pigging me up. He might just as well stick two hands all the way down his throat and squeeze the last ventricular throb out of me."

From my father's death I learned adversity, and adversity, like experience and Miss Davis, is a good teacher. From experience you learn that every cloud has a silver lining. Arteries, however, should be lined only with their quick, moist, supple selves. No extraneous matter for an artery, or it will tell that sturdy heart of yours. And hearts need arteries more than they need rest. This, Miss Davis, you failed to tell me, this I gleaned along the way. The Fleischmann's pamphlet has a colorful drawing of an artery filled with cholesterol. The artery is a nice glossy pink, the cholesterol is dark as motor oil, thick as birthday cake. It lies there, making it tough on your blood. Now, this blood is bothering nobody, minding its own business, carrying some good nutrients here, a few waste products there. Blood is congenial. It is the symbol of Brotherhood Week. The body's own little whore, it goes to any man. The Red Cross takes blood from you and gives it to someone who needs it more. The Red Cross is like Robin Hood; and blood, Dr. Shimmer, we know it as a self-evident truth, blood is better than money. In the pamphlet given free by Fleischmann's margarine, a cutaway drawing shows the cholesterol in peaks and valleys, like flames nipping at the blood as it goes through a narrow place. The definition of a hero: Someone who defends a narrow place against great odds. This I learned from Dr. Arthur, English 201. Not as valuable as Miss Davis's dictum on rest, but still, what is more heroic than the heart defending a narrow place, the quickly clogging artery? The odds against the heart are literally infinite. Still it works; it puffs itself up, it goes overtime, it seeks alternate routes—the smaller country arteries where the traffic is lighter, but in a pinch. . . . And if the heart, defending the closing artery against the odds is heroic, then get this Dr. Shimmer, Dr. Arthur, Miss Davis, Frieda still in grief. Get this everyone who can use it: Of those who die each year, more than half are the result of heart ailments. And each one of these millions died a hero's death as surely as any Norseman of old who wanted Valhalla enough to stick a dull knife into his chest at the first sign of sickness.

"Why look for other heroes," Howard Cosell says, "when right in front of us we have this eighteen-year-old kid with the knife scars of the barrio barely healed upon him, this eighteen-year-old who tonight showed us what manhood was all about. Did he back away from spades with knives? Not this kid. Hard as nails. He listened to his manager. He watched out for low blows, and punched from the shoulder. I'll tell you something, folks," Howard says, "this is off the record but you

9

know I'd like to see the day that Johnson and Mc-Namara and Rusk and all the rest of them get into trunks and come out in the open to spar a few with Ho Chi Minh, Brezhnev, and Mao. Ira is nobody's fool. You might laugh at him for tying up with Latinos and Italians and black men in this brutal sport, but who's to say that it's not the wave of the future."

Ah, the future, Howard, if only you're right about that. That is what Grandma wants from me. The grandchild in my loins and the girl somewhere in the crowd, if only the future would bring those elements together and make of them a little boy in a skullcap carrying a *siddur* and moving in silent prayer beside Grandma. If the future holds such a phantom, Howard, then it's better than championships, better than big cash purses.

"Get some zip," Grandma says, "before cancer and arthritis put me underground. Find a girl. How hard can that be?"

Harder, Grandma, than training a graceful middleweight; although in this case, thanks to Jesús, these things coincide. What I have not yet seen in a girl I dare approach, I see at once in Jesús: the elegant virtues of nature. He has everything. But middleweight contenders are not an item born, otherwise every strong misfit in Detroit might step through the ropes of the Motor City Arena to capitalize on his brute force. No, in the ring it takes more than strength, more than meanness. Jesús is not even especially powerful, not at all like the tattooed men who move refrigerators for a living or the muscle boys who glory in their triceps. No self-consciousness for Jesús. He takes his body for granted. A swift combination is as instinctive to him as reaching for a handkerchief during the pollen season is to a hay fever sufferer. The eye spots an opening, the fists are there before any other part knows what's happened.

But even when you start with everything, as Jesús did,

there are still months of learning before the swift puncher can cross the ring to meet his equal. Jesús has the rhythms of a winner, but only in short spurts. He throws three swift punches, then drops his arms. He has a tendency to look around the room, so that a fast punching bag gives him one for one. His brilliant speedy jab Jesús throws with his wrist alone, neglecting to add the sweet kiss of power from his left shoulder.

Sometimes after a long day among the batteries, radiators, and burned-out car bodies, Jesús and I barely have the energy for two hours at the gym. On those days when we're both tired, or at the times when Jesús is too lazy to skip rope or hit the bag, or too sure of himself to put on the protective cup or the headgear—at times like this I wonder why we keep at it. I consider the odds against glory, the uninsured risk of cuts and broken bones. Then I think of the reality of me at the scale weighing lead, Jesús in the yard smashing batteries. When we are down, Jesús and I read each other's moods.

"Madison Square in the spring, boss," Jesús says, and I arise from my stool. He can relieve my melancholy by shadow boxing, by dancing in the ring without lifting a glove against his sparring partner. Yes, to encourage Ira takes little, Jesús, only a few flashes of your brilliance, but how can I translate that enthusiasm to Frieda, who trusts me with our savings although the lead market is way off?

"Ira," she says, "for you I'd do anything. Maybe this is my failure as a mother. But who can say no to a son orphaned at fourteen, and from a father like Abe? I say to myself, 'would Abe say no to him'? About a boxer he would never say no. Who would believe that grown Jewish men could be like this. Like father like son. Still I thank God that you take after him. He left us better than money. Character is what he left."

When we begin, Jesús, you are still a part of the long

11

daydream from which I cannot seem to awaken. It is this that has taken my "zip." I can't explain it to Grandma, not even to Dr. Shimmer. It's as if between me and the world there is a sheet of Saran Wrap. Through it I see everything, the way other people do, but somehow I'm kept at a distance by that almost invisible layer. Then, after watching your moves for a while, my hopes for your career seem to raise the plastic sheet like a stage curtain. With you I am ready to be unwrapped.

Still, to make you more than a sloppy gym-sparring partner takes money. An engraved robe can run $200, regulation boxing gloves are $85, mouthpieces $12.50 each. There are doctor bills and $75 a month just to hit the bag in the gym and get two clean towels a day.

You would think that nothing could be simpler than two men in the ring stalking each other. The physics is clear. Two striving to become one. Yes, the second law of thermodynamics rules the cosmos, but money rules the ring. For Frieda I try to make it look like a sure thing. "He is so good, Momma, that I don't see how we can lose. Even if he doesn't get to be champion or even one of the best in his weight class, he'll still earn his keep."

"But owning another man."

"Not owning him, just managing him, just his career. You manage him—like the bank manages your money. You don't give it to them."

But we know now, Jesús, how right my mother's instinct was. I recall your remarks printed in *Pravda* as they were translated by *The New York Times*, "The beginning of the alienation of labor is the management by one individual of the affairs of another individual." Your statement stung me to the heart. Although I never intended it to become an exploitative relationship, I see

12

now that always secretly, unconsciously, I was using you for my own ends.

And Grandma, she whom you liked best of all in our family, she calls you a shvartzer, fails to distinguish you from the noisy blacks moving into our neighborhood who threaten her as she takes her daily two-block walk with the aid of a cane which she would gladly use against the colored children who spit in her path. To Grandma you never stop being a threat. When I move you to our basement, to a cozy little room adjacent to the ninety-pound hanging bag, Grandma calls a locksmith. She bolts herself into her room. She refuses to pronounce your name.

"It's *Hayzus*, Grandma. In Puerto Rico it's as common as Jack or Bob."

"I won't stay alone in the house with a schvartzer devil." I call in the rabbi to explain to her that you are legitimate. A professional fighter. A Puerto Rican, not a shvartzer. You are living in the basement so that we can save money while you build a reputation and a career for both of us. You are as safe as a devout Jew loaded with *mezuzahs* and prayers against circumstantiality.

The rabbi, too, is suspicious. "What man keeps someone in his basement and teaches him to hit other men?"

"A manager," I say. "An entrepreneur. A potential big giver to Jewish charities."

"Notwithstanding," he says, "it smacks of the gentiles."

We descend to the fighter in his lair. Eighteen-year-old Jesús in the small, wood-paneled basement room watching the afternoon movie on a fuzzy twelve-inch Motorola. The rabbi is seventy-five. He was a friend of my grandfather, whom I never knew. He officiated at Abe's funeral. He threw the first scoop of dirt; he ac-

13

companied me in the Kaddish, saying it slowly, clearly, so that I did not miss any of those tricky Aramaic syllables.

He examines the ninety-pound bag, itself a hundred-dollar investment. He smells it but does not touch. The bag moves lightly in the air. The chain creaks. To him you are a caged animal, smooth, brown, awesome. He thinks of me as the man with the chair in the den of lions and tigers.

"From this people earn a living?" he asks.

"Millions," I say. "It is safe and clean. Policed by the state board, and supervised by doctors. There have been great Jewish fighters, too."

"Ira," he says, "your grandfather of blessed memory was a sage. He was more devout than most rabbis. Wisdom dripped from his fingertips. He died young. Your father, too, slipped into eternity in the midst of his prime. Only you has the angel of death spared. Only you to watch over the declining years of your grandmother and your mother."

Is this the only reason I have been spared, I think, only to watch over these women, not to live as Ira Goldstein, who once played in the Little Leagues and who may yet gather diplomas, women, and fortune in the wide world of the gentiles?

"Rabbi," I say, "you know that she will listen to you. Don't approve of my venture. This I'm not asking. Tell her only not to be afraid that Jesús will slit her throat. He is honest and sincere and hardworking. As soon as he earns a little money, he will move into a delux apartment. I couldn't let him stay in a single room on Woodward Avenue without even a hot plate and so much noise that he is up half the night. A boxer must guard his body. Food and rest and training—these are his Torah."

"And your mother? Frieda approves of this?"

"She lets me do as I please. Rabbi, I'm twenty-four, I'm not a boy. At my age other men are in the world in the midst of success. They have wives and families."

"So why not you too?"

"I will, Rabbi, God willing, in time I will too. But now there is this to do. When my destined bride appears, I will recognize her." I only say this to impress him, to put into my small talk the hum of predestination, the glitter of divine planning. And yet when Debby does appear to me, it is as Destiny. How you saw her, Jesús, I know not, nor does she. She remembers the rally in front of Cobo Hall, her Ho Chi Minh sign, the hot breeze of the evening—and suddenly you, helping her hold the sign aloft in the wind. And I, somewhere deep in the crowd, waited months longer for Destiny, for her whom you culled out of the protest march.

"Ira," you said, "can I use the pickup on Saturday night?" You who gave me yourself, could I deny you a truck? For you it was monasticism—the training, the running, the sleeping long. On Saturday night you had to break the bonds. I understood. I envied. I gave you the truck.

"For shame," Frieda says, "a Jewish girl. Someone should tell her father."

"Keep out of it," I say, "it's none of our business. We don't own the man. His private life is his own business. As long as it doesn't hurt his training." You are always home by midnight, up by seven, working out on the ninety-pounder. Your taped fists awaken me. I drink coffee as I watch the light sweat break onto your shoulders. You jump rope. From eight to nine you run over the freezing Detroit streets all the way to the corner of Greenfield and Six Mile Road and back. I make us a breakfast of eggs, rolls—and because of you—even meat in the morning: little kosher sausages tasting like the pork that inspired their creation.

I train you by the book, by the several books I have borrowed from the Detroit Public Library. *My Life* by Willy Pep, *The Career of a Boxer* by William and Alan Boyd, and *So You Want to Fight* by the editors of *Ring*. But there is no absolute routine. No book can read the individual body—the hungers, the instincts, the capacity for pain. To this day I wonder how I—a fan but with no experience in the ring—how I noticed in that single explosive moment with Moses Robinson all the nonphysical elements that make a winner. How did I spot your native intelligence, your ambition, your confidence—the smoldering hate which for so long lay within you?

"I do not like it," the rabbi says. "A young man like you should not dwell so close to paganism. The Romans did this kind of sport. On the grounds of our Temple they despoiled us with arenas of torture. Of this business I will not approve. But I will tell your grandmother that the fighter is no threat to her life. It is your life that he threatens."

"Even the shvartzer finds a Jewish girl. But not our Ira," Grandma says when she hears of your Saturday-night adventures. We watch *The Lawrence Welk Show*. Frieda takes a bath. I read Grandma the evening paper and call her attention to the clearance at Sears. I wonder what you do and who the girl is. You return silently. In the morning you offer no stories, no explanations, but your fists seem extra fresh. I imagine you embracing a lewd Jewess—as coy as the punching bag, as soft as the fifteen-ounce training gloves.

Grandma notices the happy couples dancing on the TV screen, and Lawrence Welk surrounded by singing sisters. "On New Year's Eve," Grandma says, "and all the other *goyische yom tovs*, Lawrence Welk brings his own family to sing and dance. You should see how beautiful they look. They hug him every minute. The grandchildren pour out of his lap. Not everyone can be so lucky."

16

No longer do you go to Goldstein's We Buy Junk and Batteries. Not there, where rust and infection thicken the air, not there do I store my investment. Grandma gradually unbolts herself and learns the difference between a Puerto Rican and a black, a nicety that I have forced upon her. "You'll see," she tells me, "one day you'll come home and find my blood on the Armstrong linoleum. In advance I forgive you for what this wild man will do to me. Can he help it? You bring a wild goy into your house, you have to expect terror."

The way you are with her, Jesús, shows me something that I admire more than your power and courage in the ring. With her you are gentle and patient. When Frieda joins me at the shop early, you carry upstairs to Grandma her boiled egg, her hot Sanka and toast. You leave the tray outside her door. You are not offended that she won't unlock the door until she hears your footsteps at the bottom of the stairs. Once she is dressed and moving around the house, she trusts you more. Sometimes together you scan the newspaper looking for sales. You, too, she has forgiven in advance.

Everything she can forgive, but not Solomon. From Grandma you learn the name of the villain, the details of his crimes. "Next to Hitler is Solomon." This I remember from my childhood. Abe used to laugh it off. He did not hate Solomon. "Competition is the name of the game. Business is business," Abe Goldstein said. Solomon's big trucks roared into gas stations, paid top price for the batteries, and left Abe only the loyal few who liked him more than a few dollars extra.

"He had it on his mind to kill your father—and he did," Grandma says. "With such aggravation who could live?"

"Don't listen to her," Frieda says, "Solomon is not such a monster. She doesn't know the whole story. The man suffers plenty."

From you he suffers, Momma, from being deprived of what Grandma and I and the battery business have every day. Was my need for money so great, Momma, that I sent you there to the pits of capitalism to barter yourself so that I could hire Miguel León to train Jesús for one month? Where I have never been, there I let you wander: to Solomon, the king of midwestern scrap. Solomon, the father of the fragmentizer. Solomon, whose machines chew up a car every fourteen seconds, whose semis and railroad cars feed the oxygen furnaces of Gary and Pittsburgh. Magnets litter his desk. Momma, in shame, averts her eyes from the girlie calendars that advertise heavy machinery. Solomon's four telephones ring blood. His pinky ring glows in the dark. An extra set of false teeth floats in a gold-rimmed Solomon Iron and Steel glass.

"Copper is dying," he shouts down the long corridor of typists and metal buyers. "The Africans are trying to put us out of business. Screw their black asses. Buy zinc from Arizona and chrome from Rhodesia. I don't want to look at copper until the price goes to eighty cents. Hide all my pennies."

"Frieda," he says, acknowledging her presence on the leather chair, "what is a diamond like you doing in such a business? Look at the mud on your shoes. You should be in the beauty shop at Saks or in your own Miami condominium. Look at you waiting for me to calm down. Look at you, a high-class widow, an educated woman, still young enough to marry, sitting in a junk-yard office."

"I want to borrow money."

"For investing?"

Frieda shakes her head.

"For taxes?"

"No."

"For retirement of debt?"

18

"For a middleweight," Frieda says, "with a brutal left hook."

Solomon breaks into smiles.

"You mean that slippery Mexican who pals around with Ira?"

Frieda nods.

"For this you come to the King of Detroit to borrow money?"

"For this."

"To keep me company at a UJA dinner you're too busy. A movie, a play, a ride in my Cadillac—all this is too much to ask from Frieda Goldstein. But if, God forbid, her son needs money to throw around on his Mexican boyfriend to buy dope and weapons, then she comes to ask. For me nothing, for him everything."

"He is flesh and blood. You're a stranger. Why do you do this, Solomon? Why do you torture me every time I see you? Can't you say, 'Frieda, I'm sorry?' Can't you answer straight like a bank or a rich *goy*?"

"How much does Ira need?"

"Four thousand now, maybe two more in six months. By then Jesús should be earning his expenses. We'll sign notes and pay back with prime rate interest."

"It breaks my heart, Frieda." Solomon lowers his voice, closes the door. "It breaks my heart to see you like this because your son isn't man enough to run his own life. A solid, hardheaded businesswoman like you coming to borrow money for a prizefighter. Who would believe it?"

Solomon eyes his extra set of teeth. "It's a strange world Frieda, *landsleit* like us, our parents from the same small town in Lithuania. If we'd stayed there and Hitler had left us alone, what would we own now between us, a featherbed and six copper pans? Here we've got everything."

"You mean you've got everything, Solomon. To us a

hundred dollars a day is still a big deal. If I had everything, I wouldn't be coming to you now for a middleweight loan."

"Frieda," Solomon says, rising from his chair, "Frieda, for you I wouldn't refuse anything. Ask for my balers, my semis, my load luggers, even my fragmentizer. Only ask and see what happens. But for your son and his Mexican, am I a crazy man, Frieda? Did I build Solomon Iron and Metal from a pushcart to an empire by handing out thousands to prizefighters? I didn't give a nickel to Joe Louis, a national treasure, when he had his tax troubles. Why should I support a Mexican who if he could get past my fence and my dogs would steal my wallet and cut my throat out. It's like giving money to the Arabs."

"All right, Solomon. Enough. I understand. I know it sounds risky. The difference is, I trust my son's judgment and you don't. Still, a secured loan is a secured loan whether it's to a Mexican or to the Chase Manhattan Bank."

"What's the security?"

Frieda pulls her diamond ring with difficulty over a swollen knuckle. "A gift from Abe in '42, when business was good for the first time in years. Three-and-a-half carats." From her purse she removes a jeweler's letter. "Appraised value, sixty-five hundred dollars, slight imperfection not visible to naked eye, blue-white pear cut, platinum setting."

Solomon holds the ring in his large red hand. "Had you married me I could have given you one of these every year, every month if you'd wanted. From a working lifetime this is all he gave you, this trinket?"

"Solomon, it was enough. Do I get the loan or not?"

"Laverne," Solomon yells down the corridor to a secretary, "come in for dictation. Eight and a quarter interest. This ring stays in my vault for security. The lawyer will send a copy."

So Abe's diamond, the only love gift you have, this you mortgaged for your son's whim. Oh, Momma, I wish I had been like other well-meaning sons who lead their parents to lose everything in the stock market or on can't-miss franchises. I wish that instead of Jesús I had met one of the imitators of Colonel Sanders, and with him led you astray more conventionally. I wish that I had found my zip and a head for business early in life. I wish that I had showered you with grandchildren and dividend checks. But Momma, I now believe that Solomon was yours as Jesús became mine.

He takes the ring from your outstretched finger. He throws it in an empty ink well. He pulls you toward him. For my middleweight, Momma, you are the collateral.

2

The path from the locker room to the canvas ring is laced with craters. A worn-out blue rug runs the length of the walk. Popcorn crunches beneath the eighty-dollar boxing shoes. Castro calls this your immersion in the cauldron of capitalism. All revolutionaries, Fidel says, make the long march. Mao's went through the mountains and along the Yellow River. Fidel himself traversed the wilds of Camagüey and Oriente Province. Jesús Martinez Goldstein, your long march is through catcalls of bored men. Some reach out to slap at your back where the tight bronze muscles twinkle beneath the robe. All around us flies the flag. Old Glory emblazoned even on the ceiling of this converted armory. The national anthem is the prayer of Jesús, the moment of silence before the pure theater of the fight takes over. Because, Jesús, once that bell rings all of our analytic planning vanishes. It is, as Fidel says, "total physics." When I read your statement that "The laws of physics rule the ring as surely as the proletariat will rule the world," I thought to myself, Is this the man who stepped through the ropes that March 15, 1965, to face Otis Leonard of the scuffed shoes and drippy nose? The crowd is with you automatically. The crowd such as it is, three hundred or so strong, is a collection of derelicts, fans and wild-eyed heroin people full of smiles. But that night I don't even notice them. It is only you I am

22

focusing upon, you and the beginning of my own long march to glory.

The curly hair of Jesús, the wily black eyes, the teeth whiter than the canvas floor, the powerful arms—all of this is visible to the naked eye. The fight fan sees more. He notices the natural footwork, the economy of movement, the power that operates all through the body and is unleashed like inevitability when it finally pushes out from the pillowy glove.

As casually as your jabs rip the flesh of Otis Leonard on that night, with that same lightness of manner you approached Debby, held her banner, whispered into her pampered ear some revolutionary slogans of your own. She recalls your speed. "One kiss and he is all over me," she says, "his hands go toward my underwear. Fighter," she says to you, "I'm not your below-the-belt punching bag."

For me you have discovered her. Just as I did the groundwork for Fidel and Brezhnev and the unnamed millions whom you will liberate, you, Jesús, find the answer to Grandma's prayers. Debby is twenty when you find her in the crowded rally. Your eye is good. She stands out. Her sharp gentile-like nose, her pale skin and the flame of her anger appeal to you. She is the kind of girl who ruined my adolescence.

"What did Plato say about screwing women?" you ask me, and then I know that your Jewish girl is only a refugee from the land of cashmere sweaters and Ford Thunderbirds, not yet ready to embrace the future in the lunges of a Puerto Rican fighter. Secretly I am glad.

"Plato believed in friendship," I tell you, "in non-romantic love."

"Bullshit," you say. For weeks the pickup stays home on Saturday night, but you roam the streets disdaining Jewesses for the light-hipped girls who do not mention Plato. You are home by midnight. As the record grows, so does the discipline. Six four-round victories. One each Wednesday night. All knockouts.

Sal Contrato, the promoter, on a whim names you Goldstein. "It might get some Jews back into the armory," he says. "They spend a lot on refreshments. When they left boxing, they took the class with them. They moved into hockey and basketball. Jews are gregarious people. They like team sports."

Some are not so gregarious. Like me, I love the loneliness of the ring, even along the apron where I await my man for the minute between rounds. But, Jesús, you are the crowd's man. You laugh at the name Goldstein, but you take it on; you let Contrato emblazon it across your robe. While Ali is beginning to inspire a whole generation of black men to adopt Muslim names, you, the middleweight hero of the people, go for the archness of a Hebrew name. All of you is contradictions. "The most versatile Communist ideologue since Trotsky," Fidel calls you, but to Grandma you remain the dangerous basement dweller, the shadow between herself and her family, the evil eye on her grandson's future.

Let me tell you about the evil eye. Yes, I know that the postrevolutionary world will have no place for such nonsense. Even in our time it has been a fading superstition, but don't forget that I was raised by your friend, Grandma. As a child I worried about the evil eye. More than polio I feared it. Because the evil eye is something that a friend, too, can throw at you in a sort of accidental way. It can be a Freudian slip with cosmic power. Suppose you happen to look particularly good some day, an acquaintance notices it. Now, he means no harm but that little voice of envy within him shoots out a millisecond of "may pimples scar him for life," and the damage is done, virtually without the realization of the perpetrator. We live in a world where unformed thoughts are as powerful as deeds. "Watch out,"

24

Grandma warns me, "for ladies with goiters, men who limp, children with running noses." And I am equally wary of the hunchback, the flea-bitten, the partially paralyzed, and the sane, whole healthy ones who say "come here little boy," and try to pinch your cheek. I am the only child of an only child. On both sides of the family. To me "uncle" and "aunt" are abstractions; my cousins collect pensions.

If you think that I hovered over you trying to protect you—my investment—from accidental mishap, imagine how Grandma guarded me from the evil eye. Until I was school age she washed my face daily in her urine, and made me swear never to tell Momma. Of course she rinsed me off with clean water, but it was there as an invisible protection against the evil eye. As I grew older I made up my own little superstitions. Various objects had powers to protect me, but I stepped on cracks in the sidewalk and walked beneath ladders. I could have broken mirrors too, if I had had the chance. With you, Jesús, I tried to keep my body from touching the ropes as I moved between the second and third strands, and I never let you touch the water bucket.

At home I insist that you eat your meals on our excellent Wedgwood bone china. Frieda rebels at first but then gives in. "Who are we saving it for?" I ask, a reference she knows to the years of frugality that earned her this china. She was so secretive—sneaking it into the house in unmarked bags, one big plate at a time—but too proud to keep from sticking the hard-won plate in that black mahogany chest with the glass doors. They called it the china closet, but to me it was the safety deposit box, the secret place in the house. When Abe carried a lot of cash, he would make a round wad of bills, turn the little key in the middle of the glass doors and drop the bills smack into the china teapot, carefully replacing its top. Every other valuable document went into those

Wedgwood dishes. My parents' Hebrew marriage certificate lay in the covered vegetable dish next to my grandfather's citizenship papers and passport, the truck title, the house deed; and, when it came in the mail, it was with pure instinct that I laid Abe's death certificate neatly beside them. The china was Frieda's only extravagance. She took pleasure in announcing the difficulty she endured to be able to buy it. She defended each piece, "I saved money all year by not letting the butcher salt the meat for ten cents a pound extra. It adds up to a few nice dishes." Each piece of Wedgwood sat on its own plastic stand. They were like green-and-white troops behind the glass doors. Before we had you, Jesús, the china closet was the last defense of the Goldstein family. When the day of judgment came, Frieda and I would open the dark doors, and with the teapot and vegetable dish leading the way, that china would march out to defend us—shielding the documents, the cash, the petty martyrdom of her sacrifices, shielding all with its power as an "investment." "Investment" still was a magical word. You, too, were an investment, Jesús, that's why I wanted you to eat your meals on those dishes. I want my investments to know each other. The fighter and the china—now that is a portfolio for all the world to envy.

And against that envy, that universal evil eye, I don't even have the strength of Grandma's piss. So I worry always, Jesús, that you will be injured in sparring at the gym, that somebody's flower pot will fall on your head and kill you along Seven Mile Road. Traffic, bathtub slips, choking, freak diseases—all these things can trip up a budding career. And we have no insurance. Frieda says, "How can you worry so about him and then every Wednesday night send him out with someone who wants to hit him as hard as he can? It doesn't make sense."

She disappears sometimes in the evening. She never

26

used to. Is it Solomon? Has my fighter's career sent my mother forever into his grasp? Jesús, do you know the family comedy? Do you know that Frieda in her late forties is still sought by our enemy Solomon? Grandma told me stories. I grew up thinking him a young rapist. When I finally saw him, he was short, bald, and toothless. Frieda could knock him out in one round.

As a modern man, Jesús, I did the best I could for you against the evil eye, but even if I were as careful as Grandma I could not have conjured a defense against ideology. I saw the stacks of *Ramparts* and *The Daily Worker* beside your basement cot. I knew that you craved the front lines of the anti-war movement, but how could I believe that your career did not come before all these matters?

Otis Leonard, J. R. Thomson, Brutus Phillips, Jordan Simms, Al Truax, Jimmy Malone—all these black and white middleweights went down like bowling pins before your onslaught. Their wives and girl friends wept bitter tears at ringside. You whipped these men so quickly that your robe barely seemed to leave your shoulders. On some Wednesdays there was no sweat on your limbs. You dressed without a shower and went home to read. I smelled Madison Square Garden or the Coliseum in Los Angeles.

Days in the battery business lost all meaning. I stopped being careful; the acid shredded my work pants and left burns upon my thighs. Grandma put aside her fears. Her arthritis stiffened her wrists. She needed you to help her around the house. She pretended you were an ordinary domestic, a *shabbas goy*, whose duty was to make her comfortable. She sent you to the drugstore for Mercurochrome and let you dab it on her nails as a remedy against the swelling. In your own memoirs you wrote, "The old lady, the grandmother, was the only one in that group of capitalistic lackeys who understood the

27

value of labor. She had no contempt for the ordinary man. Her understanding was marred by religion just as Marx points out—the Jew sees only other Jews, not mankind. Within the severe limits of her historical perspective she treated me well. The rest of them exploited my strength, she used me only to aid herself in time of legitimate need and to turn on her electric appliances on Friday night and Saturday."

All the time, Jesús, I was fooled. I thought you put up with her Old World insults and understood the trouble I had gone to before she reconciled herself to your presence in the house. The whole thing you present in a very strange way in that little book that has caused me such embarrassment. You make it seem as if I even stood in the way of your political education. You say that I censored your reading material, and yet all I did was look for big print to protect you from eyestrain. "He never inquired of my plans for the future," you wrote. "He treated me as if I was a piece of machinery which, with good care, might return an astronomical percentage on his investment. A speculative but fairly substantial piece of capital goods." And what you say about gangsters, this makes no distinctions between the Mafia and Solomon and me. While it was going on, you were deadly quiet. Only the murmurings about Plato as you whacked at the big bag outside your bedroom door gave me an inclination that Debby was disturbing you. Everything else you kept to yourself until the Kid Sangrilla fight, and by then you were big news and beyond my power to direct.

It is true I went to Debby as a pimp. I was fearful. For all I knew she would resent me at once. Even her address would have been enough to scare me away in most circumstances. In six years of night school I had never visited a student apartment. From the classroom to the pickup to home was my route. Those happy people going out for pizzas and throwing Frisbees to each other were no friends of mine. They even carried their books differently. Until I became your manager I held no hopes to compare with theirs. You were my equalizer. For your sake I went intending to plead with the girl to loosen up, to forget Plato and think about the middle-weight championship.

You were already picked as a comer by *Ring*, had eleven impressive wins, and were almost ready for a solid diet of ten-rounders. But I noticed that your defensive moves were slow against Truax; and Malone, your eleventh opponent, landed a right cross on your chin that put you on the canvas. You went down like butter melting. I had to fight all my instincts to keep from jumping into the ring to pick you up. Of course your showmanship and power saved the moment, even turned it to your advantage. You shook the bewilderment out of your curly hair, beckoned him with an open glove and then pointed to the spot near the far post where, with one vicious uppercut that reminded everyone of Kid Gavilan's bolo punch, you put Malone away. The *Free Press* printed that picture of you pointing to the spot. "Just like Babe Ruth," the caption said. But while the sports page touted the uncanny accuracy of your prediction, I went a few blows back to remember you stunned, on your back, looking for help in the empty air. Yes, I worried about my investment. A loss could set us back months, maybe forever. The crowd likes consecutive strings; it is the no-hitter psychology, the vision of perfection. For this I risk a meeting with the girl who I think has perhaps slowed you down. With difficulty I pry her address from you.

For my own sake and for Grandma's entrance to eternity I do not seek out the lairs of Jewish girls. But for you, my investment, my Puerto Rican middleweight, my silent star to be, for you I overcome shyness, put beneath my arm a folded copy of the *Ring* issue that lists you, and climb her stairs.

Devastation hangs from the walls of Debby Silvers' living room. Ho Chi Minh and the red banner fly amid black-and-white snapshots of napalmed children and griefstricken mothers. Legless refugees sell souvenirs. She sits on a water bed eating M&Ms. She reads a book called *The Structure of Music*. At once I recognize that she is the end of my quest. She beckons me to her water bed, the only furniture. I tremble with lust. For a momment, Jesús, I forget you. Her brown nipples cast shadows through the soft Indian shirt. Her thighs flower in blue jeans.

"I am the manager of Jesús Goldstein." She laughs at my formality.

"Ira, I know all about you." She smiles but her look is fierce, as if the atrocities upon the wall had been performed upon her parents, yesterday. She moves barefoot through the clutter of her room to make instant coffee.

"I, too, am against the war," I tell her. Her entire body grows rigid.

"I can't talk about that. I have to read my Aesthetics assignment. If I start talking about it, I can't make myself study. I just want to go and sit in front of the White House and fast until they stop it all."

I thumb through *The Structure of Music*. I tell her that the only music I really listen to is the sound of the bell at the end of a round.

"Don't make light of yourself," she says. "Jesús tells me you have been like a brother to him, and saved him from the viciousness of life on the New York streets."

Why didn't you include that in your memoirs instead of that portrait of your manager as a vicious capitalist? And if you didn't believe it, why did you tell Debby and predispose her to liking me? Had you told her I was a reactionary, there is no doubt you would have ruined my future.

Perhaps the angels intervened on my side. Those same angels who helped Dr. Shimmer deliver Frieda from danger, those angels who were at the side of his forceps during that long, hard labor that extracted me and that makes me feel guilty. "Twenty-two hours," Grandma says. "Abe went to shul to say psalms." They added another Hebrew name so that the angel of death might be fooled. And out I popped, worth every second of that agony, and the angels go to work immediately seeking out a bride for me. They have a tough time too, these angels. Grandma knows. In this respect her stories are not different from the fairy tales of the gentile world. There I learn about fairy godmothers who concern themselves with the individual welfare of a wretch like Cinderella. From Grandma's stories I know that the weaker angels, the ones not busy guiding the events of the wise men, these concern themselves with finding proper matches for young Jewish men and women. These intervening angels, and not lust or money or congenial personality, determine our brides. They check history for mates. They work under severe limitations. Life is short, the fertile season shorter still. They are limited by geography and most of all by the small number of Jews. "What if the angels accidentally find me a *shiksa?*" I used to ask.

"Spinoza," she said. "This one will grow up to shame us all. In the other world I'll be forced to avoid the glory of the Lord because this apostate is growing into a wild Yankee. *Shiksa feh.*" She spits. I grow into the age of wet dreams, never daring to ask again about the possible mistake of an angel. The evil eye I know I'll recognize should it come at me through the layers of urine, but a young gentile woman? How, after all, will I be able to

31

resist that? I know, Grandma, that the Holocaust should weigh heavily on me. I know what losses we suffered. But really, what bothers me the most are all the Jewish brides that perished before the angels even had a chance to evaluate them. I was born on Pearl Harbor Day. While other Americans sat silently beside radios, shocked and afraid, Frieda screamed for twenty-two hours in Butterworth Hospital, screamed at the indifferent nurses already busy with Jap hating, screamed at Abe, at Grandma, at Dr. Shimmer himself, who later enlisted in the reserves and pranced around the clinic in khaki on Thursday afternoons.

Grandma's theory is that I was deposited extra deep in Frieda because of the danger of elevators. Now, the Jap and the Nazi—these dangers she did not comprehend. But a crowded elevator at Hudson's and her Frieda big with child and carrying the pressure cooker that they bought on sale to steam my baby vegetables, this is a danger that even the angels can't protect from. The elevators can make you vomit with their speed, but worst of all they expose the big belly to elbows, shoves and "Excuse me, I want out here" on every floor. Handbags smash at Frieda, briefcases, umbrellas. Grandma is all hands trying to protect me from these elevator strangers. And until I see Debby on that water bed, I have done nothing to repay that prenatal care.

So thank you Jesús, and thank you, angels, for not leading me to shiksas; and though Debby claims to be a nonbeliever, for Grandma's purposes she counts. Still, here I am confronting my destined love, and what do I do? I try to convince her to be "good" to my fighter, to stop bothering him with Plato and start doing what radical girls are known for.

She laughs at me. "I've seen *The Great White Hope*. I know that women can ruin the careers of big black brutes. You want me to screw him, Ira, is that what you have come here for?"

"No," I say, "of course not." I hope that the angels are not listening. With such a frank tongue how will she stand beneath the *chuppah* surrounded by flowers and beaming relatives? Still, I get a hard-on. The embarrassment alone is enough to make me flee.

"Ira," she says, "don't run away." She holds my hand, keeps me on the water bed. "Jesús told me you are shy, lonely. I know the risks you take on his behalf. I know that you borrowed money from Solomon. I know who he is. In high school I went out a few times with Darrell, one of his sons. He had a mania for bowling. On our second date he bought me a big black ball with my initials on it. I refused to take it, and I thought he would cry. Everyone knows what a bastard Solomon is. His own sons hate him. To be in debt to him is like mortgaging yourself to Satan. Jesús appreciates what you are doing. So do I.

"You know, Ira," she tells me, "I am not a pacifist, only a protester against this war. I believe aggression should be released in a healthy way. For Jesús, the ring is healthy. As far as the sex goes, he can take care of himself, you don't have to help him out. He talks about Plato because I am trying to educate him away from hard-line Marxism toward a more general utopian theory."

This is the first time that I hear about the Marxism. To me you never say a word. Of course I guessed—and so did Frieda—that you probably had a reason for leaving New York, a police record, an involvement in dope or numbers. But who in 1965 thinks of Marxism? You are an anachronism, you belong in the fifties, though then as a middleweight you would have had to take on Tony Zale and La Motta and Sugar Ray himself.

"What do you mean by his Marxism?" I ask in honest innocence. "He wants to make a million in the ring."

"Don't be so sure, Ira. There are things he would not compromise." From her I learn some of your story. Your birth on the Island in poverty. Your mother's escape from a cruel husband aboard an Eastern Airline's flight full of carefree tourists. Her marriage in New York to Diego Martinez, who began by organizing popsicle cart pushers, and rose to power in the International Socialist movement. "His stepfather spent most of the fifties in jail. Jesús grew up around freethinkers. He met Norman Thomas. But due to circumstance they neglected his education. What he knows are propaganda tracts. He honestly believes Gus Hall will someday be elected president."

"He never talks politics to me," I say, "only boxing."

"I draw it out. I am interested. He thought because I am in the movement I am one of them. I was sure he had told you."

So, I thought to myself, my middleweight is a Communist, so what? Also, I thought, it comes full circle. Grandma too palled around with the Communists, the more serious kind in Odessa in 1917. Before she married Zayde she knew the boys who wanted to change the world. "Communists, Zionists, freethinkers of all kinds," she said, "wanted to marry me and take me away from the righteous path. My father chose for me. He picked your grandfather Meyer, a Talmud *chochem*. You could burn the whole city of Odessa around him and if he was reading about a section of Torah, he wouldn't notice anything else."

So, Grandma, two generations, a war and a continent later, one of these Communists catches up with us. In fact, on Wednesday nights we own him for up to thirty fighting minutes. This is what America means. Everything can happen here.

"I didn't mean to betray a confidence," Debby is saying. As she moves closer to me I think not of Marxists but of those nipples only inches from my arm. This, or perhaps the word Communist itself, brings back to me the memory of the one sexual pleasure of my life: Sharon Shapiro on that night in October when President Kennedy said he was going to stop the Russians from putting missiles into Cuba. If only every day brought threats like that one. Sharon Shapiro stood up and screamed in the Italian restaurant. The owner said, "The President is going to speak," and he put on the TV. I could still eat, but not Sharon Shapiro, my blind date, the niece of Sylvia Karp. Sharon Shapiro of Briarwood, Illinois, I hope you are not reading this. It was my good fortune to be with her for the apocalypse. She worked on JFK's campaign. She had a framed letter of thanks. She was virtually going steady with an anthropologist from Harvard.

"It's war," she sobbed aloud, even though the President asked us to remain calm. She ran to the pay phone to see if they wanted her back in Briarwood, Illinois, for these dreadful hours or minutes that might be everyone's last. Her father, a lawyer—a calm man whom she trusted—told her to stay put at Aunt Sylvia's, he would call her in the morning. "If there is a morning," Sharon Shapiro said. She had no time for lack of intensity. "When the end of the world may be this close," Sharon said, "we cannot guard our emotions. Think of how terrible it must be for him."

With JFK, Sharon Shapiro suffered. She could not look at her spaghetti. Decisions had to be made. Khrushchev counts his missiles, looks over his grandchildren, contemplates the gleaming walls of the Kremlin, and decides that Kennedy, after all, might be the greatest fool in history. The Russian destroyers glide serenely toward the Caribbean, their sailors vaguely aware of the American F-4s flying rhythmically through the clouds as if to lead the way toward the island of happy brown comrades.

President Jack and brother Bob come in from playing touch football in three-hundred-dollar suits. They huddle in the White House. Jackie, still pale from her miscarriage, cancels engagements: "The President and Mrs. Kennedy regret to inform you that because we may be momentarily involved in World War, we will be unable to attend the opening at the Museum of Modern Art." From the Kennedys she learns that catastrophe is no excuse for rudeness. Sharon thanks the waiter, checks her makeup in a pocket mirror. Jack and Bob, Dean Rusk, McNamara and the joint chiefs stay put in the White House beside ticker tapes and twenty-foot maps of the earth laid out flat and calm as if by a pre-Columbus cartographer.

While John F. Kennedy and Nikita Khrushchev face each other across a dark, lonely ocean, like lovers competing for the fertile little slit of Cuba lying beneath her bearded master, that night Sharon Shapiro—who hardly knows me—takes between her drawn lips my moist phallus. "Before we are cast into the oblivion of geologic time," she says, "I want to try this. About this I have always been curious. Let me."

Oh, Sharon Shapiro, I let you and I thank you, and I excuse you now and in the thousand times that I have relived that moment.

"I should have been with David tonight. What happened should have happened with David."

Yes, I believe you but maybe David doesn't deserve everything. He must have you now. You returned to Illinois the next day and never even sent me a note. Sylvia Karp told me one day in the supermarket that you were married. Since on that night you could not blow your David or John F. Kennedy, so you did me, there on the edge of the universe in your Aunt Sylvia Karp's recreation room. If I would dare to tell Grandma about this, I would ask her if the angels were finally getting around to doing their job for me and were testing a few models before making their decision. I don't honestly know if I am a virgin as I sit beside Debby on the water bed. I have never asked about the technicalities. Sharon Shapiro seems like a war experience. That night she had me too believing that the mushroom-shaped cloud coming up from Miami would be our last vision. "Detroit is a primary target," she reminded me, "an industrial center. We may be the first to go. But what difference do a few minutes make."

So, I think it is as an almost complete male virgin that you find me, Debby, panting upon your water bed. The procurer become the seducer.

From Sharon Shapiro I have learned that at the world's end people dabble still in idle curiosity. Socrates, at the end, said he owed someone a chicken; and my own father, more humble than Socrates, said, "I'm hungry." Oh, my father, I know what you meant but the nurse didn't. While you grabbed your heart, she left you to fetch skim milk from the pantry. "He said he was hungry," she told Dr. Shimmer, who excused her literalism.

"It's all right, Nurse Phillips," Dr. Shimmer told her, "he didn't know what he was saying, a dying gasp." Dr. Shimmer fills out the morgue forms. I am fourteen, looking down at my silver ID bracelet, at the big solid square letters that say IRA. Twenty feet down the hall Abe is laid out. Nurse Phillips gives me his teeth and glasses in a clean white envelope. I take them home. I never tell Frieda or Grandma, who have forgotten these trinkets of daily life, but I still have my father's upper bridge and his bifocals in my desk drawer right beside Webster's Dictionary.

"It's late," Debby says. "Have you accomplished your mission? Do you still want me to go to bed with your fighter? Or," she asks, reading my look, my hunger, as Nurse Phillips failed to read Abe's, "would you rather keep me for yourself?"

You, Debby, are no Sharon Shapiro. Not for you are coyness and curiosity. You are as straightforward as a Cliff's Outline.

Across the water bed you come toward me. You kick off your sandals so they won't weigh you down. I feel as if I'm twenty feet deep in that bed. I sit expectantly, the way kids do at the bottom of swimming pools waiting for the buoyant water to lift them to fresh breath. When you kiss me do you know what I am thinking, I am thinking "enough, this is enough." There is a Hebrew song, "Dayanu," recounting in a folksy way all sorts of miracles and the chorus sings out after each one, "Dayanu" ("It would have been enough"). The lyrics mention the crossing of the Red Sea, the gift of the Sabbath, the splendor of the Ten Commandments—each one would have been enough. The chorus would settle for a gesture, a promise; the chorus could have withstood, if necessary, another thousand years of slavery in Egypt. And for me, too, Debby, it would have been enough if you had only kissed me the way you did while I sat there still holding *Ring* magazine in my sweaty left hand. You could have licked your lips with your small tongue and waited for me to try something else. Or you could have said "it's wrong," or "I hardly know you," and still I would have walked away from your apartment grateful and fulfilled.

It would have been enough, Debby, if having kissed me and then having moved back to look me over and assess the effect of yourself upon me, it would have been enough if I had seen only that saucy teasing look come over you, that smile that said "Lucky Ira, I'm going to get you. You're as trapped here as the sufferers on the walls. Lie back and enjoy it." That look alone I enjoyed more than anything I had ever seen. I would not have traded that look and the sense of anticipation that it carried with it for the combined favors of all the Playboy bunnies of all time.

When you reached down to pull *The Ring* from my grasp and tossed it carelessly on the floor, then I knew for sure that it was not just kissing but everything. And once my hands were free of the boxing magazine it was as if every thought of Jesús went with the magazine into the rubble beside the bed.

My hands, Debby, my hands knew what to do. With Sharon Shapiro I remember that they didn't know. If I had put them on top of her head it might have embarrassed her or caused her discomfort. And using them to grab some part of her seemed wrong. In fact, only her back was available to me while she bent into my lap. I remember putting my hands on her Aunt Sylvia's tweed couch, which was rough and uncomfortable.

But for you, my destined one, the hands knew more than I did. Before the rest of me, the hands got zip. Maybe these hands know the difference between passion and curiosity. For me the second kiss, the feel of all of you pressed against me, the motion of both of us upon the waters—this too would have been enough. But the hands are going everywhere, to the breasts, they go. . . . Enough. I am thinking this is enough. Then the belly. Okay, enough, and those fingers, like tourists, shop along the wide boulevard of the thighs. My mind is singing "dy—dy—anu, dy—dy—anu," the Hebrew ditty of modesty; my eager hands are dancing to a wilder rhythm. Finally, the Dayanu voice blends with our movements. The mind keeps on with this song, but it is no longer the one I chanted at the Seder between the second and third cups of wine. In the midst of Dayanu, a small miracle happens: Zip passes through me, and it is not merely the charge of sexuality. In fact, if I were not so busy I would stop to wonder at the appearance of such a thing. That my body could go through the proper motions, I had always known, but whether my mind would let it, of this I wasn't so sure.

It might have happened in other ways. I could have experienced such euphoria in the middle of a mathematics problem or while reading a poem or even while watching a boxing match. But as a special sign, as if I needed it, through you, I discover zip. The mind and the body together, this secret pleasure I learn from you on our first night. Grandma, I thank you for praying that I might acquire zip, and Debby, to you I am forever grateful for this moment. But zip, I learn, is not a steady thing, not like money in the bank. "It's called postcoital depression," you say as I lie there contemplating what must be a turning point in my life.

"Whatever you call it," I mumble into your shoulder, "Dayanu. It's enough."

3

My draft notice sends Grandma packing. You, Jesús, carry the old trunks down from the attic. "My great-grandparents were Russian citizens," she says, "they'll take us back in a minute. We've still got friends in Odessa. But you, you'll have to stay here. Only relatives can go back with me. In Russia their fighters would kill you. They have big Kalmuks from Siberia. They fight with whips, not like here."

If Grandma only knew whom she was snubbing in her desire to save me by getting back to Russia. "Anti-Semitism everywhere," she says. "Who ever heard of Vietnams, and still they're after Jews."

Frieda is more practical. While Grandma packs for emigration, she goes to Dr. Shimmer for certification of my marginal high blood pressure, my flat feet, and my hay fever—wild around pollen counts and sure to blow the whole army out of Vietnam when I start sneezing in the jungles.

But with Debby Silvers at my side I go the hero's route. Hundreds cheer. I like it, I know how Jesús must feel. I hold my draft card aloft, Debby raises the Zippo lighter. "Hell no, we won't go!" young men behind me are chanting. Memorial candles are the only light as we stand ceremonially in front of the library beneath a soaring American flag. It feels like Yom Kippur.

For the sins of Johnson, forgive us, O Lord; for the

41

sins of B52s, and marines—yes, even for the sins of good intentions and for the sins we have not committed but only thought and for the ones we have not even thought. For everything let this Zippo lighter atone.

And also for sins I am committing upon the girl with the lighter—if in this age these are still sins—forgive these too, Heavenly Father.

I hold the card until my fingertips crackle. Those Buddhist monks who burn themselves alive are for a second my fellowship of pain. Debby sucks my fingers. You, Jesús, ignorant of what I am doing, are asleep in your cozy quarters. To you I am now a deceitful master. Because of her I hide my private life. I leave you alone except for our daily training sessions. "Tell him," Debby says. But I cannot risk her, not yet. If I have to choose, it is her, not my middleweight. Fame and fortune can go out the window.

But you hardly notice my new life. Since the Babe Ruth–like incident you have become the dandy of sportswriters. They call almost every day. They stop in at the gym. Bill Green of the *Free Press* calls you "The Crab" because of the way you tend to jab with an almost open fist, as if you would rather claw and snatch. The name sticks. Like Goldstein you laugh it off. All things come easily to you. "Bring on the champion," laughs Crab Goldstein. "I'm ready for everybody."

Then the arena closes. While I am up in the air with the draft, fearing Canada may be my only alternative, Sal Contrato decides Motor City Auditorium is his living grave. He wants the stock car racing business with his brother-in-law. "Shit, this is Motor City ain't it? We'll give 'em motors. Boxing is as dead in this town as a good whorehouse, when all these broads are giving it away. In the forties your boy would have drawn a paying crowd to training sessions. Now they want football. Let fucking Henry Ford give 'em football."

"Sal," I plead, "what about Jesús coming into his own? Where will I book his fights?"

"Take him to Vegas. There's still a little action there, and if things don't work out, a fast Mexican can earn plenty as a pit man." For the first time since I imagined you in the ring, my hope honestly falters. When we needed money for a real trainer, I didn't hesitate. I asked Frieda to go to Solomon. For a month of Miguel León, the prince of trainers, she risked her diamond. For my whims as a manager she risked the scorn of her lady friends. Bad enough that the mother runs a battery junk yard, the son takes up a new business—a boxing manager. Some family. Would you believe they're only two generations from rabbis in Vilna. Only three generations from considerable money in the timberlands of Russia. Whose daughter would you wish upon such people? When finally there is a daughter ready to risk it and opponents primed for ten-round main events, Sal closes the Detroit market. This is monopoly power out to get my Marxist. In a free economy we could fight on street corners and charge onlookers the way kids sell lemonade.

Jesús, my creation, what could I do? If I had not felt guilty for taking somehow from you, although accidentally, your Platonic woman, I might have let it all go at that moment. But I thought I still owed you, and I did—even now I'll admit that. I owed you the chance you had earned with your fast hands.

For you, I stayed with boxing. For me, my mother went finally to Solomon forever.

4

"Peace, peace," Solomon said, "there is no peace." All six of his phones rang, their lights flashed in the air. To his right a ticker tape whirred out metal futures. When Solomon was down, not even the thought of 1929 could make him answer the phone. Secretaries, buyers, transportation officials all sat in the waiting room. Busy men across the country were put on hold. "To have all this," he said aloud, "and yet die unfulfilled."

"Please, Mr. Solomon." Through the oak door came the voice of Maureen, his executive secretary. "Please just see Mr. Sanderson. He came from Toronto. He has to catch a noon flight back. You made the appointment months ago."

"Throw the son of a bitch out," Solomon roared through the door, "Throw them all out. I'm closed for the day. Can't I take a rest? Even the goddamn computers break down." Maureen cleared the waiting room and the phone lines. She opened the Muzak speaker to his office. Solomon took the pillow from his closet and lay down on his Brazilian leather couch.

It was 1936. Frieda had graduated from high school, wore her hair in a tight bun. She lived above the bakery and carried its aromas with her. *Challa* in her smile, sugar donut lips, Solomon hungered for everything. He bought fresh bread before each meal in the hope of ei-

:her seeing her come down the outside wooden staircase, her legs in colored hose, a book in her hand, or seeing her during her working hours, surrounded by the rolls and cookies, measuring out with those small and beautiful hands the pounds and dozens. Through the glass case Solomon watched her crisp movement. On Saturday night he waited for her until eighteen minutes after the sun set, and they let her out. She had to be home by midnight. In the summer the sun didn't set until nine-thirty. All week he daydreamed about their two hours together while he ran the scale for greedy Epstein, who cheated every peddler.

They were landsleit, he and Frieda. Both born in Detroit within a year of the time their parents emigrated from Russia to Michigan. His family were freethinkers, as happy to escape Jewish ritual as Russian persecution. The Weiners never strayed from orthodoxy. Detroit was Gehenna to them. They even applied for return visas to Europe but cousins dissuaded them, brought them dishes, pots, chipped in to help open the tiny bakery so old Weiner would have his own shop and not have to work on the Sabbath. Their only child, Frieda, they raised like a memorial candle to the old ways. Her innocence glowed. On Saturday she wore long white dresses. Even as a child he loved to see her walking down the street beside her stiff black-gowned father.

When they passed Solomon, old man Weiner spat. He hated the Solomons from the old country, where they were pariahs and he a prince of the synagogue. Their equality in America he did not recognize. Little Frieda looked on in shame at her father's rudeness. Solomon fell so deeply in love that he longed to have a Bar Mitzvah, to win her by skillful Biblical paraphrasing or whatever it was these people valued. His own father raised him to be a socialist and a universalist. Solomon often told people that if his old man were alive he would be mortified by his son's success. "A pinko to the heart," Solomon said. "We sat home every night waiting for Revolution just like the religious Jews awaited the Messiah. By the time I was a teen-ager I knew that money was all that mattered. His universal socialism never got him more than nine dollars a week. But I think even my father, who lived for his ideals, could have been bought off for a fifty-dollar bill. I don't believe anyone ever gave him the chance."

In school when he read *Romeo and Juliet*, Solomon knew that Shakespeare spoke only to him. He wrote her long love letters in badly spelled Yiddish and English. He longed for friends like Mercutio, for meddling clergy, for anything that might bring him close to her. When she was sixteen, old Weiner died, stiffened in his regular chair at the synagogue. They knew he was dead only because he failed to stand at the appropriate moment.

Solomon waited out the mourning time and thought he had a chance. For a week Frieda cried. For the next month she would not smile. For a year she heard no music or idle talk. When she was seventeen he proposed wildly as she tried to run away from him down a Woodward Avenue alley. He caught her behind the Florsheim Shoe store. Their feet were in a small mud puddle. With two hands she still held her long skirt aloft for the run. Against the dark, wet bricks he pressed her, laid his lips to her chin, to her neck. She stood motionless, terrified, expecting Satan to leap from the eaves trough. Solomon cried, mortified himself, lay down in the mud, promised suicide if she spurned him. He was wet and muddy. Frieda laughed, ran from him to the sunlight of the street. "Don't chase me into alleys," she called back to him, "Come to the house like other boys. Momma will let you."

For another year he courted her on Saturday nights. Other men wanted her. Every week brought new

46

matches offered to her mother. Money was theirs for the choosing. A big clothing store owner wanted her for his son. A pharmacist with four stores, doctors, lawyers— everyone who saw Frieda wanted her for his own or for his son. Without old Weiner to guide them Frieda's mother wavered among the suitors. "Meyer didn't care about wealth," she said. "He wanted a good family. Even as far back as the great-grandparents. If possible, he wanted rabbis on both sides of the family. I'm just an ignorant woman, how can I choose the right man for a girl like Frieda?"

While Bertha wavered among the choices for her daughter, in her heart Frieda chose strange, wild Solomon, a confessed eater of pork, an offspring of wild atheists, hardly more civilized than a gentile. He followed her through the city. She felt his dark eyes always looking at her. At home, sometimes, through slits in the window shades, she suspected him. He alone of all the suitors dared to kiss her, touch her. He had nothing to offer. Only his passion, his youth, his possibility. His own family laughed at him for courting the one they called the "Queen of the Jews." His father, the socialist, taunted him. "They'll have you grow earlocks yet and run to the synagogue three times a day. You'll forget the working classes. The world is full of women. Pick someone who will be a help in the class struggle. What can this silly girl do, pray?"

Solomon was prepared, if asked, to adopt her gods, her ways. For her he would change his dress, his manner —anything. One Saturday afternoon as he stood outside the bakery awaiting the setting sun, hoping for an afternoon glimpse of her, he saw her mother go out with a group of women. He heard them talk of an afternoon with sick Mrs. Rosen. They wouldn't return until evening. He tortured himself by waiting an hour, then rushed up the wooden staircase. She awakened from a

47

nap to open the door, asked him to leave; her mother would find out, neighbors would see. She blocked the door with her body. He brushed against her as he moved through. From downstairs, from the cold ovens came the aromas of yesterday's dough. Frieda herself still pink and warm from sleep let him enter the room, forgetting for a moment the monumental risk. In her presence Solomon was all instinct. His hands moved toward her. Talk was superfluous.

"No, Solomon," she said. Her father's spirit hovered. She pummelled the back of his head with her soft slippers, scratched at him—but not with all her strength. Her father's treasure, the Queen of the Jews, was just an eighteen-year-old high school graduate who secretly practiced the Charleston, who wore lipstick and the kind of underwear her mother didn't know about. If she lacked Solomon's intensity of passion, her own was still sufficient to the task. They fell to the ground, her flannel nightgown, his gabardine suit, wrinkled in embrace. His cufflinks tickled her ears. Her father's soul howled from the grave. All these months she had avoided with her mouth those lips that she knew to be unclean. She suffered his kisses upon her cheeks, but now her lips, too, he touched and the soft flesh of her neck and breasts.

"Meyer called me from the grave," her mother said later. "There I was sitting at Mrs. Rosen's bedside when I heard Meyer say as clear as I ever heard anything, 'leave this old lady and go home to your daughter.' "

With the outer door not even closed she found them locked in embrace. Bertha poured the hot water from the tea kettle on him, burning too the exposed breast of her daughter, making him scream more for having to part from his beloved than from pain. With the tea kettle still aloft, she chased him down the stairs. The neighbors saw.

"Nothing happened, Momma," Frieda sobbed.

"Harlot," Bertha called her, not even offering butter for the burned bosom of her only child.

In fasting and in penitence and in pain Frieda stayed in her room until Monday. The rabbi knocked at her door. Abe awaited her in the living room. They tied knots in a handkerchief. No gifts were exchanged. Abe had rabbis on both sides of his family, although he himself had no particular gift for scholarship. Solomon knew him as one of the peddlers whom he regularly cheated at the Epstein Brothers scale.

"In such a way your father made a choice for you," Bertha said. "He warned me that if I did not do the duty of a parent you would end up like the beasts."

In a small and quiet wedding ceremony, Frieda circled her new husband seven times. He was a big, slow-moving man. Rabbinic blood had not made him argumentative. He too had been born in the New World, in Detroit. For their honeymoon he took her to Navin Field to watch the Tigers and the Yankees. Although she always remembered her guilt about that Saturday afternoon, Frieda did not regret her marriage. She loved Abe Goldstein and the sweet slow-moving son who so much resembled him.

Solomon left Detroit the day of her wedding. He hid outside the synagogue thinking that even at the last minute he might murder the would-be groom and take his place. No one noticed the spurned man. He took the first bus to the east. He stopped at Pittsburgh because he was carsick. For a year his own parents did not know his whereabouts. When he returned to Detroit a decade later, rich and arrogant, his heart was full of vengeance.

He married Irene Kay—her real name and her stage name. She sang at the piano bar that was Solomon's first nighttime stop in Detroit. He ate a heavy beefsteak, drank wine, watched men and women on the dance floor. Irene Kay's silky voice moved them. He liked her leaning over the piano with a microphone in her hand. He had checked the credit rating of Goldstein's Batteries & Scrap. They were not even listed.

"A fucking peddler has my treasure, and all my money can't do anything." He sent Frieda a letter telling her he was back, offering to give Abe $25,000 to let her go.

"My dear friend," Frieda wrote to him. "It is my pleasure to see you have so much money. In these days who has money like that—only you and Rockefeller. The knowledge of your success makes me happy. I knew you would be a successful person. Although Abe is not successful, we have, thank God, enough for our needs. Please don't think about me and what might have been. This is a closed book. Each person goes the way of destiny. Mine is Abe, yours is riches. Marry someone soon. This will calm you and keep you from loneliness in your old age."

He sent a waiter with a note and a hundred dollars to Irene Kay. The next week they were married. She bore him three healthy boys. He built a house in Sherwood Estates with a nursery for the children. Irene Kay lived in splendid isolation. When she died, the boys went to boarding schools. Summers they travelled or lived at camps or dude ranches. Solomon paid all the bills and required no post cards. They led their own lives and rarely saw their father. Two of the boys were married and ran one of Solomon's companies. He never visited his grandchildren.

Frieda pushed past the secretaries.

"Mr. Solomon won't see anyone, I'm sorry."

"Solomon!" Frieda called out as she knocked. "It's Frieda Goldstein." He opened the door and spit hot phlegm at his secretary.

I can hardly stand telling it. Thirty years late, Solomon gets what he wants: my mother. She comes in to plead my case. They can't advance their fighter's career without a local arena. How can they go somewhere else? The thought of Ira and the fighter alone in Las Vegas makes her shiver. They also have no money for this. He breaks down. Frieda holds him in her arms. His silent ticker tape, his unlit phone lines, and his warm tears move her. They bump against the desk, scattering ashtrays and magnets.

"My life is cursed without you," Solomon says. "It is one long day, these thirty years. I earn these millions to keep myself from falling apart." She notices his big soft earlobes, the age spots on his hands. Her own breasts sag in his arms. She has trouble catching her breath from his kiss.

"Life catches all of us," she says. "Abe never got the chance to watch me grow old."

"To me," Solomon says, "you're still the Frieda upstairs above the bakery, the bride I never got."

"I've got varicose veins, now, Solomon, and spots of battery dirt here on my index finger that nothing seems to wash out. And Momma is old and hates you as much as ever."

He hugs her as if she is a cashier's check.

"Once you got away, and look what happened to me."

"What happened to you should happen to everyone."

"Not the money, everyone thinks only of Solomon's money. What do I care for the money, strange *goyim* will spend it when I'm dead. Yes, that's what my sons are. Bill and Bob and Darrell—even the names are strange to me. They're big and blond. They drink beer and go to church on Sunday. What can I say, they're good citizens, but from me—from my heart and my blood—they took nothing."

"Solomon," she says, "how can you say that about your own sons?" She is thinking of me, Ira, the little

51

jewel of her body, the reason she and Grandma keep going on cold dark days. Me, her sweet Ira who is about to be drafted into the army. To Frieda you can't say anything bad about sons; she holds up her Ira as if he were St. Francis. Just to be a boy is nothing. A son, that's something. Ira became a real son young, while others were still boys being boys. He wore Dad's watch, his Masonic ring, his gold tie bar. He tried to lower his voice and steer the car underhanded like Abe did. A boy imitating a dead father—there's a touching thought. And this boy, this *mensch* who honors his mom and grandma —him they're going to send to Vietnam.

"Not if I can help it they won't," Solomon says. He takes Frieda's two hands and leads her to the plate glass window at the rear of the office. The King of Detroit Scrap, emerging from his own dark melancholy, is strangely gentle. In silence they watch the slow grinding force of the fragmentizers. Cranes hang at odd angles over hundred-foot piles of refuse. Half-loaded railroad cars litter the landscape.

Oh Momma, I understand what must be happening to you. Suddenly in his office, looking out at the empire of rust, you have a vision of what life might have been. A life of your own balers and semis, of secretaries engraving checks, of cheerful good mornings from employees, and conversation with customers who are not drunk or exhausted.

I had the same hopes for you, Momma, only they were to come true from my efforts not from Solomon's. I would rise from tending the scrap yard to a position of power and brilliance in the world. It's not such a wild fantasy. Every day on the Johnny Carson show aren't there actors and writers and other stars telling us how they rose from humble origins to become what they are now. I have been working, Momma, these six years in night school to make something better of myself. I know you don't want me to work like my father did. "Ira has Abe's personality," you say, "but God willing he'll have better luck in the world."

Grandma says your luck is determined at birth, and my birth emerged out of torturous labor, shrouded from the world by Pearl Harbor Day. Could there be anything lucky about such a birth?

"You can never know," Grandma says, "you just have to wait." So I wait through six years of night school, dreaming that I will be the first medical doctor or supreme court justice or international businessman who has ever gathered all his knowledge and diplomas exclusively in night classes. "Yes," I will tell Johnny Carson, "I missed some of the fun, some of the social life that day students probably experience, but none of that really bothered me. In my youth I was not frivolous. I wanted to become something so that my mother would be able to retire from the scrap business and my grandmother could have some pleasure in seeing our family tradition of excellence emerge again after a lot of setbacks on this continent."

"He's not just anybody," Grandma says at my graduation. "After all, look who his grandfather was." She is the main speaker at this event. All of the important people at the university have given her this exceptional honor. It is their way of being proud of me. I stand among my fellow graduates, all of us as tired as if we were in class, most of us a decade or two older than regular graduates. Our ceremony, too, takes place at night.

Grandma wears academic robes which are only slightly fuller than her black dresses. A few thin hairs appear beneath the mortarboard. I am number one in the class. Xerox and IBM send telegrams competing for my services. Their personnel managers offer me blank checks. "Fill in any amount," they tell me, "any amount.

Don't be shy. We can't do this for everyone, but in a special case there are no rules." Even the Detroit Tigers try to lure me back to sports with a bonus of $50,000 and a guarantee of no minor-league play, but I'm already in my mid-twenties, too old for games. "You should have offered when I was eighteen," I tell the GM, "then I would have signed for peanuts. Years of night school take a lot out of a young prospect. I don't have my old speed or reflexes. Now instead of playing for the Tigers, I'll just invest wisely for a few years and then I'll buy the team."

Grandma is impatient with all the sports talk. "Bring in the businessmen," she says. "Not in public, not at graduation," I say, "wait at least until the ceremony is over."

The president of the university gives Momma and Grandma honorary diplomas to thank them for all they've done for me. Together the three of us march down the aisle. "I should only live to see the wedding," Grandma says.

Yes, it is my wedding she is awaiting, Momma, not yours. My rich spouse, my worldly success, my offspring —you, Momma, are the lost generation. Having delivered me and then suffered your own bad luck, you have been moved out of the path of our family's destiny.

But luck still plays her own tricks. Grandma is right, everyone has to wait. There in the enclosure of his fortune Solomon stands ready to tear asunder once and for all the three of us as we await my future.

The tears stream down his tanned cheeks. Your brown work oxfords, Momma, have left grease stains on his carpet, your boy's windbreaker makes noises against his custom-made suit. Yours is the success story, Momma, yours the rise from humble origins. There on his Brazilian leather sofa high above thirty-three acres of recycling equipment, Solomon fulfills his dream of you.

The crane operators lean out of their cabs to observe their boss in ecstasy. Millionaires from all over the country continue to wait for Solomon to reengage his telephone. This time Grandma has no premonition. This time, Momma, you are old enough.

5

Caluccio Salutatti, in Detroit on Party business, read the obituaries at the end of the sports section. Across from the deaths, Caluccio looked at the picture of the smiling Crab Goldstein raising an Everlast glove. The Party had never gone in much for sports. Entertainers were better educated. But since the end of the blacklist days entertainers had found new causes. You could comb Hollywood and not find a Communist. And the new-style radicals—most of them thought Stalin was a German. Everyone was looking to the East these days. Vietnam, Thailand, Burma, China—these were your hot spots. Caluccio missed the good old days when people worried about losing Europe. He had spent some months in jail and a lot of years on the road. In Belgrade, in Prague, in Sofia, in Warsaw, he could be greeted by important people on the street. In Detroit he was just an old man in a shiny suit.

"Sonofabitch," Caluccio murmured in his native Italian, "if that ain't the Martinez kid." Professional Communists never forget a face. That is one of the things that goes on in cell meetings. J. Edgar Hoover knew this. They spend twenty minutes of every meeting on memory practice. They try to meet in rooms with lots of angles, with pictures on the walls or exotic surroundings of some kind. They prefer old buildings. They train the mind to associate, to put today's secret orders mentally on, say, the dirty wastebasket in the corner. If they are ever captured and grilled, they are taught to remember single items rather than the entire wastebasket. It is an old trick. The Dale Carnegie people teach it to executives. Salutatti was a master of memory. He saw the picture of Jesús Goldstein, recognized it and brought to mind the entire Martinez file. He allowed himself to say aloud, "I wondered what happened to that kid." Caluccio stayed in a cheap hotel downtown. The FBI watched every step. He went to a pay phone to call the *Free Press* for Goldstein's home phone number. Caluccio wondered what the kid was like, wondered what part of the old days had rubbed off and whether the kid, in spite of everything, had kept some ideology. "He's still got that baby face, like his mother. I'd know him anywhere."

"Jesús Martinez," Caluccio said, when the fighter came upstairs to answer his phone call. Grandma watched with obvious suspicion. "You remember Caluccio Salutatti, Caluccio with the safe house in the Bronx?" The fighter broke into warm smiles of recognition. "I haven't seen you since you were maybe ten years old. Has it been tough on you, kid? I'll bet so. You know none of us ever forgot Martinez. There's a fund and a scholarship in his name. The rest of the barrio ain't fit to shine his shoes. They deserve what they're getting. I'm glad you think so too."

In the course of the conversation, Caluccio dropped some signs and coded messages. The fighter responded to several in kind. "He remembers something," Caluccio thought, "maybe Martinez did not die in vain." They arranged to meet at the zoo in front of the elephants. Jesús could be doing roadwork. It would not look suspicious.

With pain, Caluccio allowed himself a rare moment for a working Communist organizer. He allowed himself to remember the inglorious end of fellow worker, Sylvester Martinez. For a while Salutatti and Martinez were partners the way Jack Webb and Ben Alexander were in *Dragnet*. In light moments Martinez actually called Salutatti Sergeant Friday. Sometimes, they cruised the east coast in a '56 Ford. Salutatti specialized in small Italian businessmen and organized labor. Martinez had the more difficult work of organizing the immigrant masses pouring up from the Island. They had a tiny budget. The FBI men who followed them could afford the Holiday Inn across the highway from the nameless roadside cabins they were forced to choose. And Martinez's own apartment—what a living chaos. His wife's two children from a first marriage, six of his own from several women, and assorted comrades or just down-and-out Puerto Ricans who came to Martinez for help. Fast Spanish talking filled the apartment day and night. The kids ate and slept on the run. In the squalor important decisions had to be made.

Martinez, his belly too round for a belt, snapped his suspenders against his chest as he considered options. "Salutatti," he used to say, "you, with a big quiet house in the Bronx, you can afford to be philosophical. Here, I got to make judgments every five minutes. Not everything can be pure. Here, Lenin couldn't think so good either."

Martinez, in delusions of grandeur, thought of himself and Salutatti as America's Lenin and Trotsky. He thought that when the time came, the government would send him in a sealed train from Harlem to Washington, D.C. He would go on all the networks and declare martial law. People would stay home while all nondomestic property was seized. In a few weeks they would organize parades in every major city. Reformed capitalists would march arm in arm with workers they had previously exploited. Martinez and Salutatti would organize a new and enlightened government. There would be no secret police, only an army well trained against counterrevolution.

"Martinez, you dreamer. Not in our lifetime."

"It's what keeps me going," the heavyset Puerto Rican told his partner. "If I didn't have the living example of Comrade Lenin I too would go to the church along with my poor brothers who do not trust me when I tell them the world is theirs."

In the house of Martinez, in the hope of revolution, in the midst of Harlem, Jesús "Crab" Goldstein reached boyhood, learned his politics and his fast, shifty footwork. He was the eldest stepson, the offspring of Maria and Rodrigo Sanchez. Maria left Sanchez in a drunken stupor on the Island, fled with her two small sons to New York. She met Martinez. He took her in. There was no official marriage, but everyone knew her as his wife. The FBI was upset that her welfare check went to a Communist organizer, but they were powerless. Every month they watched the signature, hoping to put Martinez away for forgery. Maria knew no politics and little English. She mothered her own boys and the Martinez group of six neglected ones. She tried to clean up the apartment. Salutatti remembers the softness of her skin, a tiny, frail woman who smiled much in spite of the hard times. Salutatti used to bring them leftovers on Monday from big Italian meals.

On the weekend Martinez had chances to make real money on numbers. People would have bought anything from him. He was a neighborhood leader, but the fat Communist would not let organized crime near his doorstep. When nine-year-old Jesús once hit a number, Martinez locked him in the closet for a whole day. He wanted his children to grow up untainted. He wanted them to be able to hold up their heads with pride in Moscow. Every Friday they took baths and put on clean clothes. He made them shine their shoes. They stood against the wall at attention. Then they practiced walking up Ninety-sixth Street pretending it was Lenin Square and they were on their way to the Kremlin. They marched to the storefront which Martinez called his lecture hall. On Friday afternoons he spoke to a few dozen —the faithful. The FBI men waited outside. They admired the nice, clean habit of a family walk.

Jesús never learned to read too well, but he knew the catch phrases of the revolution. He knew what "symps" were, and he awaited the dictatorship of the proletariat. He daydreamed of being a socialist realist. He spat at churches and felt a personal obligation to steal hubcaps and, when possible, radios from all Cadillacs, Buicks, and Chryslers. Jesús thought Moscow must be as easy to get to as Connecticut. Since coming to New York he had not travelled farther than Salutatti's house in the Bronx. There, they gathered once in 1952 to meet Jean-Paul Sartre and Pierre Legois, who were in New York to address committees of the United Nations. The war in Korea was booming. Five-year-old Jesús heard that Eisenhower had of late become a fascist. Martinez did not like the French comrades: "They talk too much," he said. Young Jesús noticed their lightweight suits and the way they made big motions with their hands. These two Frenchmen were the first slender comrades the boy had seen. Everyone who came to Martinez's apartment seemed to be trying to match Martinez's weight as well as his ideals. Salutatti had a backyard with fruit trees. The boys picked some apples for the skinny Frenchmen. Jesús kept a few for his mother. When Martinez saw him holding back on his gift, he quickly accused the boy of accumulating capital. "To each according to his needs," he lectured to his stepson, "you know that."

"Mama needs too. She is as skinny as they are."

Martinez slapped the boy. "Your mama is skinny by choice. Big meals sit all around her. These men lose their appetites with hard work for the Revolution—they read books all day and night. Their eyes are weak. Their stomachs too. Give them the apples." He turned Jesús' pockets inside out. Two small apples fell to the ground. Sartre picked them up and carried them to the thin Spanish lady on the sofa. He kissed her on each cheek.

"If he weren't a comrade, I would have thrown him out the window," Martinez said on the subway ride home. "He wanted to make me look like a tyrant. They are trying to do the same to Stalin. In France, nothing is honorable."

Salutatti, who loved his partner's dedication, knew there would be trouble with the family. A man who gives his life to the Party can't have a wife and six children. Salutatti had aunts, nieces, nephews. This was plenty. Martinez did not agree. "The family is the microcosm of the State. Before there can be a just State there must be a just family. Before there can be a just family there must be women and small ones."

Martinez wanted them to learn Russian, but he did not know it himself. Maria tried to practice good English. She studied grammar books at home with the children. They did not go to school. Martinez and the Board of Education were in the midst of a legal suit. He did not want his children to pledge allegiance to a government he did not support. Salutatti thought it a silly issue. The Party would have preferred Martinez not to press it. He persisted with a legal-aid lawyer who hoped for a career with the ACLU.

On the streets where Jesús Martinez spent his days and some of his nights nobody cared about his stepfather's politics. Jesús had two gifts: speed and peripheral vision. He could see so far around himself that nobody dared come at him from behind. His fast hands pummelled boys much bigger than he was. Jesús never lost a street fight. He could feel safe without a knife.

61

Mama was proud that he went weaponless, that he joined no gangs, that with her he tried to practice good English. She wanted Martinez to send all the children to school, but she had no strength to argue with him. His whole business was arguing. People came from the Bronx and Brooklyn, from other states, from Cuba too, just to argue. Maria kept out of his way. He grew heavier and argued more but made fewer demands on her at night. She prayed that none of the children would become drug addicts or Communists. Martinez did not allow her to go to church, but to herself and for her children she prayed every day. She loved them all, his and hers alike, but Jesús was her pride. He never complained. Too little food, too little sleep, not enough attention from her—nothing seemed to bother the boy. He was quiet but jovial. He learned early to stay out of Martinez's way.

After school he worked in the supermarket. The manager said a boy like that would be a store manager himself someday.

Concerning the end of the Martinez family, Caluccio had heard several reports. He was out of the country so he could not be sure about the accuracy. There was a speedy trial that involved no politics. Maria's first husband, Rodrigo Sanchez, had also come to New York. He lived as a petty thief for several years before he spotted them one Friday afternoon headed down Ninety-sixth Street for Martinez's lecture. He remembered the slim thighs of his wife, the warm sun of Puerto Rico and their innocent days as fourteen-year-old lovers. He immediately hated the fat one who marched ahead of her. He eyed the line of children not knowing which were his. Maria walked with her head down and did not see her former husband. Sanchez watched as they sat in the last of the four rows and listened to the fat one talk to them and a few others. He followed them to the Amsterdam

Avenue apartment. The family took off their Friday afternoon clothes and hung them in their one closet. Martinez too removed his lecture suit to replace it with his size fifty-six bib overalls and flannel shirt.

Sanchez wanted his wife and sons. True, years had passed, but blood is thick. He came in to demand. Maria and Jesús were in the bedroom going over the helping verb "have." Martinez was snapping the bib of his overalls. The other children had scattered.

"My wife and my sons, fat one!" Sanchez screamed, bursting into the room. "My wife is mine and my boys for my old age. Turn them over." Martinez did not know the man. He had forgotten Maria's other husband. All children were the same to the Marxist, his own or someone else's.

Sanchez, full of drink and possibly heroin, waved a pistol. Martinez thought he was one of Franco's fascists out for revenge. In unison Jesús and his mother were saying, "I have learned and shall have learned." When Sanchez burst into the bedroom, Maria too failed to recognize her young husband in this dissolute gunman. He threw himself at her as if in love. Martinez rushed in. The gun went off several times. Blood lined the floors, stained the shoes of Jesús as he ran next door for help.

The Party did not replace Martinez among the Puerto Ricans. They wrote off the whole minority as a bad investment. Maria died clutching her grammar book. Sanchez was sentenced to two life terms. At twelve, Jesús was without a mother and two fathers. The State offered to put him in a year-round fresh-air camp and teach him a trade. He disappeared, returning eight years later as Crab Goldstein.

6

My mother, you who for twenty-two hours screamed at my birth, who for nineteen months nursed me close to your heart, you who shared with me alone in all the world the blood and body of Abe Goldstein—you now go over to the enemy, and in the wake of your defection there my fighter and I linger. You say you did not convince him to buy Motor City Auditorium, he wanted it as a tax shelter. You say the exclusive right to promote Jesús that was part of the package did not interest him. You think it is just a coincidence that suddenly Solomon has become my Master. He who might have been my father. You are now putting him in that position. Yes, Grandma told me everything about you two long ago, before my Bar Mitzvah.

Grandma tells me fewer stories now. She is concerned mainly with her hair. For years it has been thinning though it is barely gray. She wraps it in a bun that keeps disappearing. Gradually you see more and more of the bone comb, less and less of the hair around it. Pink patches of scalp peek out everywhere. She cries about her hair, shows me pictures of herself with thick black curls.

After Grandma's bath, Momma tells her about Solomon. Grandma splashes around like a seal for about twenty minutes, then Frieda or I help her out. Her arthritic leg is not strong enough to trust. When I help, I avert my eyes. She covers herself with a towel too. Of forbidden spots I see only her smooth elbows and upper arms. Grandma's dresses are wrist length and high-collared. In Europe she would have worn a wig. Her single concession to the twentieth century is to abandon the wig. But as her hair dwindles I think she may yet go back to one.

Grandma has rules for everything. For bathing the water has to be almost to the top of the tub, and there must be a towel to sit on, so you don't slip. And there has to be a very fine Ace comb to lace her scalp after washing the hair. This is to get the lice out. On a freight train during World War I Grandma got lice. For the next half century she scrapes her scalp in memory.

She comes out of the tub all pink and perspiring. She sits in her bed propped up by the huge feather pillows she carried across Russia and then shipped, along with herself, directly to Detroit. Neither Frieda nor I are allowed to do any of the maintenance work on these pillows. Grandma makes the cases and the inner linings herself. She pounds them fluffy every day, and once every few months on dry sunny days—with great effort —she puts them in the yard for fresh air.

"With the right pillow you'll always sleep well," she says. She laughs at Americans who lay their heads on foam rubber or cotton or dacron.

After the bath, when she is warm and comfortable, is the best time for stories. I bring her hot tea with lemon and preserves, and she is ready to tell me all. Most of the Solomon stories I heard after baths or on nights when the thunder woke me and Frieda let me go to sleep with Grandma. For the rest of the night I was comforted by stories of the thundery nights in Lithuania when the straw roof leaked and sometimes the animals had to get right in the house with you.

Freshly bathed, her sore knee wrapped in flannel, her

fingernails painted in dull Mercurochrome, propped up by the pillows that she knows are the secret of rest—at times like this Grandma is a powerful being. Her frail, old body is covered and comfortable. Her voice coming out of the bed is strong and young. Her stories are full of hate.

The night Frieda tells us about Solomon, Grandma and I are looking through the *Detroit News* spread on the blanket before her. It is nine p.m. Jesús is already asleep in his basement room after an eight-mile run in cold weather and a high-protein supper. Grandma is thinking of rubbing a little bit of petroleum jelly onto her hair to see if it will help.

When I see Frieda's face, I guess what she is going to tell us. The hints have been obvious to me but not to Grandma. Frieda's eyes are red, her fists are clenched. I wish that I could make it easier for her, but, though I will be silent, she knows I am on Grandma's side. The tears come before the announcement.

"I'm almost fifty years old, Momma, already ten years a widow. The man loves me. He has loved me for years. He's not what you think."

Grandma collapses into her pillows. Her pinkness vanishes. The *Detroit News* falls to the floor. She does not say anything.

"Nothing has to change for you," Frieda says through tears.

Grandma pushes her blankets down and with both hands tears a large rip in her nightgown as a sign of mourning.

"I'm doing it, Momma," Frieda says, "no matter what." She runs from the room.

"Thirty years later," Grandma says, "the old shamelessness returns. Meyer, don't blame me. See," she says to me, "he's pulling my hair out every night. Next it will be my skin."

Her hair in the next two weeks falls away in clumps. She is completely bald and will have no wig. She covers her naked scalp with a red bandana.

Solomon, coy and rich, comes to court Grandma. He brings her a three-year subscription to the *Forward* and an illustrated prayer book from Jerusalem. "I'm an old man too," he says, "let me have a few years of peace on earth."

Grandma takes off her red bandana, shows him her cracking, bald scalp. "Lice and vermin," she says, "the two of you have destroyed my thick curls. I go to the grave like a man."

"Listen, Bobbe," he says, "I'll get you wigs from Paris, France, and Chasidic dresses to cover your neck and elbows. In my house you'll eat the finest kosher off Limoges china. For Saturday shvartzeh maids will pre-tear your toilet tissues, lights and televisions will be off throughout the house. I'll have rabbis come every day just to keep you company, and if you want Israel, you can go any day of the week. If I ask, the prime minister himself will meet you at the airport."

"Vermin," she says, "away from me." She covers her eyes with her sleeve.

"Bobbe," says the steel man, "Solomon is not used to begging favors. In the world I give orders. Strong men run at the sound of my voice. But you don't know, Bobbe, what it's like to want. For thirty years I fall asleep every night saying to myself, 'Frieda.' When the boy was little, I used to have my driver take me around and around the park just so I could see her face while she played with him in the sand. My anger I took out on Abe. Who could blame me? He had her, what good was my money? I gave up; I married a shiksa. In her arms I thought of only Frieda."

"Stop," Grandma yells, "infidel. Companion of Satan."

"Hear me out," he says. "You, whose righteousness has driven me to be a tyrannical millionaire—against you I hold no anger. I was young, I should have waited a few more months, then I would have had her. So for those few minutes of folly, I waited thirty years. Only Moses had such patience."

"You are to Moses," Grandma says, "like a flea to the Statue of Liberty."

"Now, when I am old and have long ago given up, she says, it is time. She tells me this. Ask her, Bobbe, Frieda herself. Ten years a widow. She could have had me any time and now, suddenly she is ready."

I listen from Jesús' basement room where the two of us are packing his bag. Solomon is sending him to train at a run-down resort in Mt. Clemens. There are hot springs where a few old people still come for the baths. Solomon owns the resort, a dining room ringed by cabins. There are less than sixty guests. He will build a ring in the casino and convert one of the cabins to a steam room. Jesús can run his ten miles in peace along quiet country roads. As they discuss water temperature and swollen joints, the few arthritic Jews who can't afford Miami or Hot Springs will suffer one more indignity—a boxer in their midst.

To me, Solomon has tried to be reasonable. "I'm going to help you with the fighter," he says, "and after that you'll have a job for life. Don't worry, it will have nothing to do with my sons and you don't have to like me either. Just don't torture your Momma, it's enough that your Bobbe is doing it."

I can't look him in the eye. I just hear Grandma saying for all those years, "Next to Hitler is Solomon."

What if Hitler, back from Argentina and newly rich from land and cattle, wanted to promote Jesús. Would I let Hitler, too, say to me, "Sonny, I never meant your father any harm. He was not an aggressive businessman.

68

Even if I had left his customers alone it wouldn't have made any difference. Some people are just not cut out for the business world. Now, Abe, he would have been fine working for someone else. It's like your Grandma says about you, 'no zip.'"

And all you men of affairs—I think of all of you Hitlers and Solomons and Johnsons—what have you gotten us with all of your fabled zip? You've bled Europe and Asia.

"Not I," Solomon says, "I've made honest millions in the scrap of the Midwest. And all I ever wanted was your mother."

"Jesús," I say, "what do you think of our promoter and the luxurious training camp that we'll now have?"

"Fucking warmonger," Jesús says, punching the big bag and bringing a new wail from Grandma upstairs.

"Old lady," Solomon says, "cursed be your curses if you don't let your daughter marry me and live our last years in peace and plenty. Because of you acid has eaten away the gloss of her fingernails and hard grease is embedded in those dear hands. Because of your stubbornness the boy has become a laggard, a manager of fighters, a ne'er-do-well, an ambitionless softy like his father."

"You shouldn't dare to mention his father's name," Grandma says. She winds herself in her gray shawl crocheted by Aunt Sarah with the heart ailment. She hides her face behind it, as if to shield herself from the words of Frieda's suitor.

"Thirty years ago I should have come to you and said, 'I'm taking her, that's all there is to it.' But I was afraid—who knows of what. I was just afraid. And you stole her away, leaving me bereft in my young manhood."

"Out of my house, parasite and blasphemer." Grandma looks for her walking stick. I hear her scuffling

69

on the floor above me. I want to help her. I want to go up there and hit him in the soft belly. "This one in memory of my father," I'll say, "and this one for Grandma." When he's down, I'll kick him in the false teeth. Grandma will go for the butcher knife and cut him ear to ear. But I haven't got the zip. I stay downstairs. As I listen I instinctively clutch the hand of Jesús. Now that Solomon has taken my mother, this fast-punching middleweight is my comforter.

"Bobbe," he says, "while you have been hating me for a few seconds of lust, I have bought banks and insurance companies. And without my donations that little hovel of a synagogue you go to would have closed years ago when the city first declared it a fire hazard. Wise up, old woman. Your daughter wants me now. She wants to step out of this dingy house, out of the griminess of her tiny battery shop, out of her nickel-and-dime existence into everything I can give to my new wife whom I have loved and desired forever."

"Better to be dead," Grandma says, "and have for company the bare earth than to live in Miami Beach with you, a blasphemer and the offspring of generations of atheists."

"So for the sins of my fathers, for this too I am responsible. Not just for what I had to do to make a living in this jungle but for what some peasant ancestor pulled off in southern Russia in Abraham Lincoln's time, for this too you blame me."

"For everything," Grandma says. "You and Hitler."

"Then sit in your own stink, old woman. Frieda is coming with me. Already she is at my house in the master suite, surrounded by maids, furs, and French perfumes. She sits in all this splendor crying for you, so I came here hoping you could be reasonable. But now, rot here if you like. The boy is going to be busy with his fighter. The battery shop she's already closed. Sit here

70

all alone and mourn your hair, foolish woman. I'll give you one last chance. Do you want to be in the Jewish home? With one phone call I get you a private room and guarantee a kosher salt-free diet."

"A pox on both of you," Grandma says. "May you have as many boils as I once had curls." She raises her stick in the air and brings it down at him. Solomon catches it and twists it loose from her arm. "So violence also the righteous perform." Across his knee he cracks the stick, her protector against the neighborhood of boys and dogs. "Rot here alone, as broken as your stick."

"Have pity, monster," Grandma wails, "have pity on this bald head. Give me back my only child." She strips the bandana from her and lays her bald head on the table. Her jaw droops, her eyes close. "Give her back or do me the favor please to chop off my head before you leave."

"Never," Solomon says. "Live long and alone and suffer for your mistakes."

When he slams the door, Jesús and I rush upstairs. I hold Grandma in my arms. Her eyes are closed. She murmurs in Hebrew to the pious grandfather whom they tell me was fierce and wise in his day.

On the couch she dabs at her eyes with the bandana, then replaces it quickly, ashamed of her naked scalp in the presence of Jesús.

"I have no daughter," Grandma says.

"You've got me," I say. She hugs me and cries against my breast. Jesús takes to our training camp resort his punching bags, three sets of gloves, two pairs of boxing shoes, and his hopes for the championship. I take Grandma into the wilderness of Mt. Clemens.

7

Of course, I have not entirely lost my mother. Even Grandma does not force me into the mourning she is now pursuing. She goes to the synagogue at seven, says Kaddish, comes home to a nice bowl of Cream of Wheat, which Jesús or I have made for her. She kibbitzes with the old folks at the resort. I never tell her that Solomon owns the place. In Mt. Clemens she thrives in the midst of mourning. It is as if she never had a daughter and was raised to spend her declining days in a fighters' training camp.

Every day Momma calls me. There are tears in her voice. Neither Grandma nor I attended her wedding.

"His sons didn't come either," Momma says. "We were like middle-aged orphans. It was a sad wedding. Ira," Momma says, "do I have to explain to you?"

"No, Momma," I say.

"Loneliness happens to everyone. One afternoon in his office when I went to talk about Jesús, it just struck me that I loved him still. It sounds crazy."

"Momma, I understand and I don't make judgments." I lie for the sake of the hours of labor, the months of breastfeeding, the years of tender care.

"You're taking care of her?" Frieda asks.

"You know I am."

"Your reward will be in this world as well as the next.

72

For what you're doing for us Solomon is revising his will."

"It's not necessary, Momma."

"But if I knew she was alone I would lose my mind."

"She's OK, Momma. She likes Mt. Clemens. She has her own cabin. In the dining room they cook for her with salt substitute. I give her all three pills every morning."

"God will bless you for this, Ira."

I hardly see Momma now. She lets the chauffeur drive her around town. She lords it over the Hadassah women who scorned her when she drove a pickup truck and earned her living in an honorable way. I think she is secretly happy to be rid of us too. After all, only Grandma and I are mementos of the past. Without us to clutter the landscape, she can imagine that she did run off with Solomon in 1936 and has been living in quiet luxury ever since. Still, I don't for a second doubt her love. She calls every day; she sends checks that I don't cash because Solomon pays all our expenses here. She probably thinks that this marriage will eventually do me some real good. Already my standing in the Jewish community must have zoomed along with hers.

But Grandma, Jesús, and I are thirty miles from Detroit. Here on the shores of Silver Lake we busy ourselves with training. Jesús and Grandma awaken at six. She goes to the synagogue, he does the roadwork. At eight we breakfast, then I plan strategy with George Danton, the Italian whom Solomon has hired as Jesús' full-time trainer. In 1940, Danton spent a year as a pharmacy student. He carries a prescription pad, though he can only write memos for liniments. He has charted and timed all of Jesús' muscle reflexes and says that he will be able to detect any slowdown in reflex action. "This way," George says, "we'll be able to save him

73

from becoming a punching bag. As soon as I see a twentieth of a second's slowdown, I'll say, 'hustle his ass out of the ring.' I'll know two years before the results start showing up in action. This is preventive medicine."

In his spare time George offers to help out with Grandma's arthritis and circulation. She has taken a few baths here since all services are free to us, but she says the water is dirty. She won't show George her head, but he says that he can, under some circumstances, coax new hair out.

"*Goyishe kop*," Grandma calls him, but sometimes they play gin rummy together while Jesús takes his afternoon naps. The three of them keep busy. It is I who have almost nothing to do. Momma insisted that we close the battery shop as soon as she went to Solomon. I think she promised him that. He wanted no reminders, especially not of her in an old pickup truck. I didn't argue. My disgust with the battery business was an old story. I gave Eli Brown, who had worked for us all these years, the keys to the office and told him he could use the land if he wanted to.

"Ira," Eli Brown says, "I'm glad you and Frieda's gettin' out of this business. It's made for a shvartzer. You just watch my black ass hustle some good money outta this."

Eli cut down at its base the old "Goldstein We Buy Junk and Batteries" sign. I remember that Abe had paid one hundred dollars for that sign. Grandma and I had walked over one afternoon, just to see that brand new emblem as tall as an office building. We both thought Abe was a successful businessman. "If not for Solomon," Grandma tells me, "we would be millionaires." Until I am eight or nine and her arthritis hits the knee, Grandma and I walk for miles through all kinds of neighborhoods. Sometimes Frieda and Abe don't even know that I skip school to take the bus with Grandma to

Hudson's, where she can spend hours in housewares looking at the cooking utensils. She picks up every pan in the display, holds it about waist high, pretending she's in front of a hot oven. She plays with them the way I pound my fist into the centers of baseball mitts in the sporting goods department where she lets me spend a few minutes on the way out.

"Cheap *dreck*," she says. "Tin." She hates aluminum, and they never have any inexpensive copper. But Grandma knows that she has the king of pots, a twelve-quart copper one "that you couldn't buy in America no matter how much money you've got." She wraps it in wax paper and only uses it for gefilte fish on Passover. Like the china, it is another of our hopeless guarantees. Grandma knows she has the best pot, but she'll only use it a few days a year. The rest of the time she has to spend denigrating Hudson's housewares. Salesladies are afraid of us. When they come to offer help, Grandma is not embarrassed to be a critic. "You should be ashamed," she says, "to offer such merchandise. In two days this will turn black. And on these, when the enamel cracks, you can poison a whole house."

We never buy anything. All her American pots we purchase for green stamps—which is my department. Grandma gets the stamps from Frieda and stores them in a big shopping bag in her chiffonier. Every three or four months, usually on a Sunday afternoon, she pulls the stamps out and I wet a sponge to paste them in the books. Since Abe gets stamps when he buys gas for the truck, we build up a big supply—about fifteen books a year if Frieda is careful to shop only on double stamp day.

And the green stamp catalogue is Grandma's favorite reading material. Unlike the newspaper, where she has to guess amid a lot of words and smiling human models at what the actual item is, in the catalogue the bright pictures are self-explanatory. For green stamps we buy luxuries. In the S&H Redemption Center she does not practice thrift; there she criticizes none of the merchandise. There, everything is a bargain. We have a Seth Thomas kitchen clock in decorator colors, two webbed lawn chairs, a hammock, a set of Rogers silverplate in a wooden case—even West German steak knives. By the time we read the small print on the blades that says "Germany," we have already used the knives and can't return them. As far as I know they are our only German item. Grandma won't speak to a Jew in a Volkswagen. When she recognizes a German car on the street, she spits.

Until I learn about the Holocaust in school I don't really know why we hate Germany, but I know that my hate is real. Hitler and the Germans killed Grandma's brother, Esserkey. Anglicized, that's me, Ira. All I know is that the Germans killed him and his wife and his five children. I don't know why or how, but two years after he is killed, when I am born, his name is there waiting for me. I didn't know that the Germans killed other people too. I thought it was only her Esserkey whose picture I have seen in a big Russian fur coat. Grandma does not forgive the Germans nor does she stop mourning her baby brother. When I learn that millions of other Jews died like her Esserkey, I don't feel any worse.

In Mt. Clemens, Jesús and George Danton are the only gentiles among the guests. For some reason these health baths became the only Jewish resort in the Detroit area. At one time they were very plush, you can see this from the ornate plumbing fixtures and the chandeliers. But the resort is now very shabby. The bedspreads are worn thin, and there is rust in the sinks. For us, Solomon makes sure the rooms have new beds and chairs.

The details of Jesús' training are still up to me, but Solomon wants him to be maintained like an expensive fighter. For this he hires George Danton, who imposes the rules of "Rest, Exercise, and No Distractions." Danton has trained many a winner and knows ring strategy, he says, from A to Z. "You got to keep a fighter away from pussy. This is one of the main things. When I trained Lazerevitch for his big fights with Sugar Ray, I used to bring him pictures of naked women. 'Mr. L.,' I would say, 'exactly one hour after you lace that coon you are going to be humping this bitch. It is all arranged, believe me. Before the iodine is dry on your cuts, you're going to be making her scream for more. I've got the bridal suite in the Book Cadillac Hotel reserved and waiting. She knows who you are; she's seen your picture in the sports page. She's as excited as you are. Believe me, big fella, what you're gonna get is worth waiting for.'

"After every big fight I always had that room at the Book Cadillac and a big, strong whore waiting for him. Of course he was too tired to do anything—except in the second Robinson fight, when Sugar Ray knocked him out in two. Even though that just about ruined his career, I sent him over to the whore anyway. He claimed it was the best piece of ass he ever had.

"You got to keep a fighter hungry. This is the whole principle. When he steps through the ropes, you want him to think that the other man is responsible for keeping him from everything in the world. You want him to think, 'if only I can deck this son of a bitch, then I can get it all—money, snatch, the easy life.' This is the psychology of the ring."

"I don't think this is the best way to handle Jesús," I

tell him. "Jesús is a smart fellow. He reads, he knows politics and women. If he wants something he'll know how to get it. He won't wait for you to promise him some after-the-fight pleasures."

"Don't tell George Danton how to handle a Latin middleweight. Who trained Issac Logart and Kid Gaston and Emmanuel Torrero?"

So I sit around the tourist cabins of Mt. Clemens and let George Danton handle the training schedule. Maybe he is right. Jesús has not complained. Here at the resort he is a lot less restless than he was in Detroit. There are only the old men and women, a few bath attendants, and the resort servants. It is a quiet life. In two months, when the redecorating of Motor City Auditorium is completed, Jesús is going to take on his first ten-rounder. Solomon has hired publicity agents who come to Mt. Clemens about once a week for photographs. He is going to sponsor the first fight on local television preceded by a fifteen-minute special on the elegance of the new auditorium. The publicity man wants to tape me telling them how I discovered Jesús, but I refuse. It must be the evil eye that I fear. I almost hope that Solomon will change his mind about television, but I know that there can be no big time without the TV. He knows what he's doing.

The publicity people say he is making the old armory into the most modern boxing arena in the world. It will be designed in a circle with the ring in the middle. The balcony will be a cocktail lounge where people can sit at small tables and look down at the fight. There are microphones in each corner so the crowd can hear the between-the-rounds talk, and the referee will be wired so the sound of all the blows will reach everyone, not just the lucky few at ringside. Girls in bikinis will disrobe each fighter and carry the round number cards. They are working on special designs for the trunks. Everything will be up to date, and they want to build up the local hope, Jesús Crab Goldstein, so that in a few months the Motor City Auditorium can be host to a World Championship.

In all the activity on the days that the publicity people and the TV crews are in camp to film, I hardly notice the old man in the shiny suit waiting for Jesús near the road where he does his running. I notice that he is dressed more formally than the resort guests, but I only catch a glimpse. At night, I drift to sleep trying to dream of Debby Silvers calling for me on her water bed; the man in the iridescent suit gets in the way somehow and scares me.

For the wrong reason, Jesús, I tremble in the cot of my tourist cabin. Get this. I think it's the Mafia. I think that young Jesús, for a grand or two in advance, has decided to take a dive. I've seen it in the movies. You'll be sorry, you'll end up as a wrestler. I'm afraid that the gangsters will come after me if I say anything. Who knows about this world of Mafia gangsters? Now if these were Jewish gangsters, like the old Purple Gang that Frieda and Abe used to talk about, then who would be afraid? Before I was born Frieda lived in their neighborhood. "They were perfect gentlemen. They didn't carry guns; they made less noise than regular neighbors." Whenever there was talk about crime, Frieda always mentioned them. It was the Golden Age of Crime. The way Momma carried on about them it's surprising that I didn't become an outlaw. If any course in school had been called "Preparing for the Purple Gang," I, Ira Goldstein, would have been the first to sign up. What they did she never talked about. But drive up on a dark night and they are there to open the car door for you. Need a blood transfusion in an emergency, the Purple Gang is there to help faster than the Red Cross. A small loan, a little food—this is the Depression, don't forget—

always the Gang is there to count on. And on the Sabbath and the Holy Days: "You should have seen them. It was like a parade. They took off their wide-brimmed felt hats and put on black skullcaps. They wore flowers in their lapels; their faces shined. You saw them walking down Livernois Avenue early in the morning and you knew there was a God in heaven. And if ever in a real pinch you needed a tenth man to make up that quorum for prayer, that *minyan*, then the Purple Gang would never let you down."

I used to think that the reason they were such successful criminals, Momma, was because God watched over them because of their piety and politeness. And, anyway, what sorts of crimes did Jewish criminals commit? They didn't murder or rob. Probably they just roughed up anti-Semites who without the Purple Gang would have roamed Detroit in those days being junior Nazis. Yes, at an early age I knew all about Father Coughlin, about the German Bundt groups and Henry Ford. Because of him our pickups were always Chevys. "Not a dollar to such an anti-Semitic *momzer*," Momma said. "Never a Ford, not even a used one." I used to daydream that the Purple Gang would one day get their hands on Hitler, Solomon, and Henry Ford, and rush them off to the synagogue all dressed up to listen to a two-hour sermon. Then, if they didn't change their ways, the Gang would do what the Gang had to do. They would do it the way Rev. Lieberman used to handle the chickens. First you say a blessing. Then you twist Henry Ford's neck back and slit his jugular until all the blood shoots out. Every chicken that I watched him slaughter for us had the name of one of our enemies. I understood history. I never used this for personal vengeance. Only enemies of America, Democracy, and the Jewish people got this treatment. I could take care of my own battles; the Purple Gang stood way back in the mountains of the thirties, like Robin Hood in the forest. When we needed them, they would strike for us. "When will there be another Purple Gang, Momma?" I used to ask her, "and where are they now?"

"Some are in jail. Some moved away from Detroit and went into other business. Who knows? I never knew any of them personally by name." But if not for the Purple Gang, Momma, what other Jewish heroes would I have had?

The Gang moved quickly against the enemies of Zion. They came out of retirement, closed their other businesses, escaped from prisons where they were unjustly held. They met in the middle of the night, not far from our house, near the bakery on Six Mile Road, the very bakery where Zeide of blessed memory once worked and where you, Momma, were attacked on that warm afternoon by the lust-crazed Solomon. The Gang meant business. "There are too many Hitlers," the Gang said. "Everywhere you look there are little Hitlers. They are ruining Abe's business, they are causing prices to rise, and coercing people—even Jews—to drive Ford automobiles. And the Jewish Hitlers—like Solomon—these are even more troublesome. Against them it's a regular civil war."

The Gang invaded Europe. They erased the numbers from the arms of the Camp victims. They resettled people by the millions in northwest Detroit and in Chicago too, on the west side in the big apartments near Cousin Sophia, where there were always vacancies because the shvartze lived so close. The original Hitler they tortured for two weeks, and, when he was dead, his eternal job was to shine the shoes of the scribes in Heaven. And Solomon, for him the Gang decreed poverty. A life of a scrap peddler and battery picker-upper. Like Abe, only worse. A life marked by many flat tires, faulty alternators, a life of much grease and little company on long boring rides. A life of no hitchhikers and all meals taken at roadside EAT signs from homely waitresses. Yes, this was the decree of the Gang. Throughout the land they dispersed. They appeared at Bnai Brith meetings and gave autographs. These were not one-sided men. They could talk about more than crime and Hitler. At the B.B. meetings they were full of warm anecdotes about the Tigers and the great Jewish slugger, Hank Greenberg.

Now, once the Gang had disposed of the Hitlers, they set themselves the task of promoting new Jewish sports talent, talent like say, Jesús Goldstein, who at least sounded Jewish and would do until a more legitimate member of the chosen folk emerged as a ranking contender in any weight division. The Gang declared that no Italian gangsters had better monkey around with this Jesús Goldstein, or else.

Ay, Jesús, it would have been so easy had only your man in the iridescent suit been an average Mafioso. But what can the Gang do with Communists? Against Stalin, against Trotsky (an enemy like Solomon), against the whole Red Army, what can even the Gang do? Had you settled for crime, Jesús, I could have helped you. I could have said, "My friend and protege, what is there to gain by throwing a fight? Solomon can pay you more than they can. If they threatened you, we could have hired Pinkerton's to guard all of Mt. Clemens. But you went beyond all of my guesses, all of my worries. For you there was only one Gang I could call on, though it broke my heart to do it. I did it Jesús because I am a good citizen. Do you know that no matter how much I oppose the war, I have nightmares about the Chinese coming in to kill us all at night. Not reasonable I know, but I was raised to "Know The Nearest Shelter." My blood was typed free of charge by the health department. I wore all through junior high a little plastic tag saying A+ that might, if the Russians bombed us, save me from everything but the fallout. I believe, Jesús, that we are living in the land of opportunity. Doesn't your career prove it? Never mind that Abe didn't get too many choices, I consider that he did all right. Wasn't he present in 1945 at all four home games in the Tigers-Cubs Series? Didn't he have ringside seats at the first La Motta-Robinson fight? Wasn't he a regular at all Union High home football and basketball games? Yes, Jesús, somehow it sank in—what I said in high school in the I Speak for Democracy contest where I took an honorable mention. It stayed in my heart. I might burn my draft card but not my birthright. Here, when there are Hitlers we know what to do. Here, you are free to be a Nazi, a Communist, a hippie, anything—only somebody's got to watch out for the public welfare. I believe it, Jesús, and no matter how many times you call me a fascist, I'm not sorry. When I found out who Caluccio Salutatti was, I called the FBI.

8

Jesús. Friend, brother, comrade—you who bore my name before the masses. You who helped me attend to Grandma; you—wide-mouthed, sturdy, quick-jabbing, hopeful prospect. You, whose fists brought me out of the doldrums of the battery business; you, old pal, I turned in without a qualm. Maybe it was the way that greasy Italian looked that finally convinced me. He lurked. He waited for you at the path to the woods, near the lake, inside his car—never where people might get a good look at him. I didn't know where you went with him or what you talked about. At the same time, I was worried about my relations to my country. Call it guilt if you want to, but burning the draft card made me feel responsible. "Vietnam," I said, "is one thing, everything else is another matter."

So who am I going to go to when you tell me proudly that Salutatti is a big shot in the American Communist Party. Should I tell Solomon—your promoter, my stepfather? How do you like that, Jesús, the first time I use that word. But that's what he is, a stepdad, a stand-in for Abe, a pinch-hitter in the seventh inning. So if I tell Stepdad he'll probably stop your career on the spot and pick up another fighter to fill his auditorium, unless Momma can stop him. And her I don't want to ask. Already I have driven her to Solomon. No more. Let her be Mrs. Solomon and live happily ever after.

Still, when I contacted the local office I never expected it to go so far. I thought that maybe an FBI man would come out to Mt. Clemens and give you a little lecture and maybe show an instructional film like Miguel León did about footwork or something else to wise you up. I didn't think they would take it so seriously. After all, what secrets does a boxer have? I just didn't want the responsibility of a well-known Communist hanging around the training camp. I wanted the FBI to get rid of him, not you.

Believe it or not, Grandma understands. "They ruined everything in Odessa," she says. "You couldn't walk through the streets without a hundred leaflets. They were worse than the Czar's men, and so many were young Jewish boys who should have been in yeshivas instead of littering the streets." She says that any Communists here must be trying to devalue our money. She tells me to call the police, but she doesn't know it is you whom the Communist is seeking. In your book you say, "The fascist police did not surprise me. I was expecting all along that they would attempt to ruin my career and to cause suspicion to fall upon my accomplishments. Nothing comes from the techniques of terror. They succeeded only in frightening my manager; the people did not succumb to the lies. Crab Goldstein and the truth proved more powerful than J. Edgar Hoover."

Comrade, I don't know about that. Hoover treats you like Iwo Jima. He comes to Detroit on an air force plane, and helicopters to Mt. Clemens. Even though I have read some ugly things about the man, I am nervous and even impressed as I wait for him in the one hotel in town. Imagine, Hoover, who knew Al Capone and John Dillinger and probably even the Purple Gang, coming to Mt. Clemens to see me just because I told the Detroit office of the FBI about the Italian. I am in the lobby a good half hour early. At this time I still don't think I am

85

doing anything to damage you. Read this, my middle-weight, don't skip here, see how it really was. Yes, I am impressed that Hoover cares about us, but I think he must have had business in Detroit anyway and is just making a little side trip to Mt. Clemens. Of course, I can't help being overcome by the attention. It's like writing a letter to General Motors complaining about your car and having the president of the company fly down to take it on a test drive. And Hoover, no matter what we think of him these days, is the epitome of virtue. Though he may be mistaken now, I remember how right he was in all the TV dramas of my youth. I am not anti-FBI on that day in Mt. Clemens, and I'm not now as I write. Events have a way of taking over. I don't blame J. Edgar.

He comes off the helicopter, rounder and balder than I thought he would be. A short old man carrying a brief-case, probably not packing a rod. He swats at a fly, shakes hands. There is no secrecy. Here we are out in the open of the Hotel Sherwood, nine empty stories in the center of Mt. Clemens, and the leader of the Free World's anti-crime forces is addressing me, a nobody.

"Goddamn," he says, "it's hot here. Haven't they got any air conditioning? The fucking helicopter is cooler than this." His three aides go to the manager to request a fan. He doesn't make any small talk. He just sits at our table looking uncomfortable. In a few minutes the three of them come back with the manager and two fans, the manager asks for and gets an autograph for his son. Hoover opens the briefcase. He extracts files. "Born 1941," he says, "Turner Street School, Union High, member of Latin Club," he reads the tiny litany of my accomplishments. Then he pulls out a huge file on Salu-tatti and shows me a photograph that I easily identify.

"What the hell are you mixed up with them for?" he asks. The papers flap in the wind of the fans. I don't

86

know why he is being so gruff to me. I tell him I'm not mixed up at all. That's why I reported it. He has not read in the record of my life that I burned my draft card, but this is what I'm worrying about. This is a federal offence; if he wants to, he can take me in right now. Imagine how it would look on the front page of the *Detroit Jewish News*, Momma, your son handcuffed by J. Edgar Hoover himself, being taken by helicopter to the federal penitentiary. There has not been an arrest by Hoover himself in three decades. To strike fear into the hearts of draft-card burners and others in the anti-war movement, Hoover himself comes out of the limbo of the bureaucracy to make this arrest. Capone, Dillinger, Bugsy Siegel and Ira Goldstein: notches on the hand-cuffs of J. Edgar.

In court they will bring up my infatuation with the Purple Gang; my desire for Debby Silvers, a known radical; and, of course, the coup de grace, my Communist associations.

"I'm not mixed up in anything," I say. "I reported it."

"Watch yourself, boy," Hoover says, "there are temptations along every road." Out of his briefcase he pulls that issue of *Ring* that lists Jesús as a contender, and describes him in one paragraph.

"Is he really as fast as they say?" Hoover asks.

"Every bit. He'll be a serious contender as soon as he gets a few ten-rounders under his belt."

"Goddamn," Hoover says.

I am trembling, afraid that he will take me in an instant, as soon as I blink or cough.

"Salutatti," he says, "is a smart cookie. We think he was after Joe Louis and probably would have had Cassius Clay if the Black Muslims hadn't beaten him to the punch."

"You mean the Communists are after boxers?"

87

Hoover smiles at his aides. "My young friend," he says, "when they say they're going to win, they mean business. Do you think they're going to win by recruiting John Does in the streets of Detroit? The top is riddled," he says, "always has been. Look at Hollywood, New York, D.C. They like to keep it quiet. Our job is to stay in touch with it. We watch their moves. We use counter-intelligence."

I feel like I am in an old movie somewhere in the tropics. The sound of the fans suggests banana trees outside. The three men in suits watching us, the brief-case, the quietness of the lobby, the serious look on everybody's face mean that the stakes are high. Hoover and his men just stare at me as if they expect me to crack in the silence and confess. "Never," I say to my-self. I sip the coke I ordered before Hoover arrived and wait for the next move.

"You like boys?" he asks.

"I like girls more," I say.

"What about the middleweight, boys or girls?"

"A girlchaser," I say, "a regular ass man, if you'll forgive the expression."

"Ever make any bets on his fights?"

"Never. I never even thought of it. I haven't in my entire life ever made a bet except with a friend, which is perfectly legal."

"You know the names of any of his other associates?"

Here, Debby, I take a risk. For you, I lie, even to J. Edgar Hoover. When they strap me to the lie detector, I will fail and probably go down in history as a subversive because I don't want them to go to your apartment and see the Vietnamese suffering on the walls. I don't want the three aides to push you around on the water bed, and slap your breasts to make you talk. It's bad enough that I'm involved, you I will protect.

88

"No," I say, "his private life, if he has one, he keeps to himself."

Hoover gets up and walks around the room. "I like these corner mirrors," he says. "In the big cities they've remodeled the hotels. You don't find places like this. If they'd air-condition the goddamn thing, a person could actually stay here."

Now it's easy to look back at Hoover and say, "What a buffoon, what a silly egomaniac." But on that afternoon in 1966, as I watch him looking at his series of reflections in the corner mirrors, I think to myself, Here I am for the first time in the actual presence of a great man. Some people are not as easily impressed by greatness as I am, but to me a public name, someone who has been on television, has a terrible power over me.

If you can be honest with yourself, Jesús, for just a second, try this. Imagine that it is not Hoover and Ira Goldstein in the lounge of the Sherwood Hotel. Imagine instead that it is Lenin and Jesús Crab Goldstein. Lenin has just flown in from Switzerland to watch you work out, and he wants some information about your manager. Aren't you a little awed by this Titan? Don't you think that Lenin in the mirror looks superhuman? Here you are a little-known middleweight sitting next to one of the great men of the twentieth century. Hundreds of millions of people listen to everything he says. Wars, kingdoms, empires fall from his pockets. He dumps cigar ash and the boundaries of Europe crumble. He writes a pamphlet and thousand-year-old churches are abandoned like fat women. Well, maybe you could resist the glance of a man like that. Maybe you, Jesús, could look the twentieth century in the face and give it a light, playful jab, maybe you could spit in its eye. I'm made of other stuff. I look at Hoover's unbelievable thickness. He looks like a small safe. His suit is that same dark green, within him are the jewels of law and order; everything that makes it possible for you and me, Jesús, to be making our way against all odds into the big time. Nobody else, not the Chief Justice, certainly not President Johnson with his big bulging ears and sloppy grin could fill me with such awe. Hoover is timeless, solid. He is not only the green of floor safes, but also of mail boxes and telephone company service vans. He exists to make sure that everything actually works. The man is hot, cranky, perhaps even unworthy of his power, but the image in those mirrors is the eagle flying right off a half-dollar. Don't forget that President Kennedy has only been dead for three years and there are less than 10,000 casualties in Vietnam and the Black Panthers are still only Oakland bandidos.

J. Edgar Hoover turns to look me square in the eye. "Son," he says. In an affectionate gesture he reaches up to put a hand on my shoulder. I can't take any more. I confess.

"In March I burned my draft card, sir." I hold out my hands ready for the cuffs. His three aides look up from their martinis, their open jackets exposing the shadow of revolvers. Hoover removes his hand from my shoulder. He goes back to the table to check my file. He glares at his aides.

"Nobody's perfect," he says. "We're lucky if we note ten percent of the burners." With his gold Cross ballpoint he writes into my file, "draft card burned." I read it upside down. It looks Russian. "Do you remember the exact date."

"March 11," I say.

How can I forget that after the burning I went with Debby Silvers back to the water bed? How can I forget the Vaseline that she smoothed on my burned fingertips kept moist in her mouth on the long walk back to her apartment. The pain was good. Burning the card was too easy. I wanted to suffer a little and to be comforted by her—the red fingertips, the white blisters, the Vaseline, the aloe vera plant she rubbed on me, the butter and then after all the ointments the smooth liquidity of herself, not like Sharon Shapiro blowing me out of apocalyptic curiosity. No, this time, on March 11, 1966, Debra Silvers desired nobody else, only me, a silly sympathetic liberal who couldn't even burn a draft card without hurting himself.

She arose from love and checked her clock. "I have an exam in the morning. Art History. I hate to do this to you, but really I've still got to study."

And while she studied Picasso and Max Ernst, I walked through the surreal ghetto of Detroit not afraid of the shadowy black men who seemed to leer at impossible angles along the cold street. This time there was no doubt. I had really done it. And, Grandma, if fornication counts a little toward the great-grandchild that you need to reach heaven, then tonight has been a momentous occasion for you as well. The angels who arrange my destiny waited four years after throwing Sharon Shapiro my way; they waited these four years because they didn't want to involve me in idle business. They wanted me to be free so that I could do a bang-up job in the battery business and bring lots of recycled lead to market.

"Take it easy, Big Shot," the angels warn. "Don't let a piece of ass go to your head. After all, you're twenty-four, everyone else starts at sixteen with shvartze whores from right in this neighborhood where you have no business walking around at one a.m. To these shvartze, all you are is a walking wristwatch. One good lay and you think you're Superman. They'll cut it off yet if you're not careful. You think because you're not going to Vietnam that they can't get you on the streets of Detroit?

91

"Listen," say the angels, "because you've got on your mind a naked girl with an art book between her legs six blocks from here, you're walking around where only a few months ago the U.S. Army had to go in tanks and shoot these shvartze just like they were Viet Cong. You want to live to have another erection, then run away from here quick."

But already it may be too late. Behind me are footsteps, the kind that have taps and high heels. I hear the sound of a leather coat against thighs. I am afraid to turn. I stop in the middle of the broken sidewalk. They take me under each arm as if they are a mother and father leading me down the aisle.

"Relax, brother," the man says. "We ain't going to do any damage to your sweet white ass." The woman who holds my other arm is tall and light-skinned. She pats my hand and smiles. They both have leather coats and are perfumed and hip. "We ain't going to hurt nobody, brother, we just saw you walking along and we thought this white boy better get some help or he might not make it home by hisself. Don't you know that this ain't open territory?"

"I was taking a walk. I burned my draft card." Yes, I blurt it out to them just as I would to J. Edgar Hoover, as if this single small act of defiance will keep them from murdering me.

"Honey, that's nothin', we burned the whole fucking town." They laugh and I join them.

"Look at you," say the angels, "arm in arm with shvartze. If this is what you wanted, why didn't you go when you were sixteen with all the other boys to the whorehouses. In those days you could find women like this one for ten dollars, and not be afraid for your life. For all these years we watch him. For the sake of his grandfather's soul we do an extra good job screening for him through a thousand applicants among women from all over the Midwest. And now when we find him one right here in Detroit, now he goes out to pal around with the pimps and their women, laughing about burning down a city where the army had to kill forty-five people before they quieted down. It was a regular pogrom and he laughs."

"Sweetheart," the girl says, "where are you heading? We are going to escort you. You're getting a safe passage courtesy of two happy niggers." They laugh but this time I don't. I tell her where my car is parked. They hold me bridegroom-style all the way. We pass other blacks. Everyone smiles at us. Remnants of the recent riot are everywhere. All the store windows are boarded. Entire buildings lie blackened along the block like rotten teeth in a mouth. My escorts rub alongside me.

"This young man been out looking for pussy. Yes, I believe this white fella is out lookin' for it." The man says this and they giggle again.

"No," I say, almost wanting to boast, "no, I was just walking, not looking for anything."

"Well, you found some pussy, didn't you, man. Well, there she is. Look on your other side, that's pussy, man, ain't that what you call it?"

She smiles and purses her lips as if to kiss me.

"What's the matter, white boy, you afraid to say pussy."

"Pussy," I say looking at her. She really is beautiful. I think of Debby Silvers—small, compact, energetic, the opposite of this tall, slow-moving negress.

"Twenty-four years he waits," the angels say, "and now he's going to do it twice in one night." And you know, I would have. If I was not afraid that they were planning to kill me, I would have invited them both to Debby's apartment and asked them to be quiet while she studied. And I would have done it again, right there on the water bed with the black girl while her friend watched and gave me advice on how experienced men who have been doing it since they were eleven operate in such circumstances. But the angels overestimate me.

"Please don't kill me," I ask her, she whom I have just called "pussy" and who clings to me in the dark street.

"Honey," she says, "I ain't even goin' to fuck you. We're just takin' a walk too. Don't be scared of us. We're the two happiest niggers in Detroit right now. Can't you see that?"

I don't tell J. Edgar Hoover anything else about March 11. But later on that night, when I was home and the fear had left me, I realized that they must have been very high, probably on heroin. They did just want to walk with me. And they kissed me on each cheek as I got into the pickup. "Lock your door, honey," she called out to me, "there's bad niggers too."

So when I tell J. Edgar Hoover that on March 11 I burned my draft card, I am only telling him a small part of the story of that day.

"You burned your draft card," Mr. Hoover is saying, "and you are the manager of a member of the Communist Party. You're twenty-four years old, are unmarried and have no previous record. You are a high school graduate and still a student."

"Part time," I tell him.

"Well, I guess the record is straight now and complete, isn't it?"

"As far as I know."

Mr. Hoover loosens his tie. He seems to feel better now that the fan has cooled the room. He sips for the first time from his own martini, which looks regal alongside my watery Coke.

94

"Young man," he says, "you've got yourself into the middle of something, you know that, don't you."

"I don't know what's going on, that's why I called your office."

"You did the right thing. You see, we knew anyway. We've been watching Salutatti for years. I can tell you at what hour of the day he moves his bowels. We knew he was meeting the fighter, but, you see, we didn't know how far the conspiracy stretched. We didn't know if you were part of it."

"I'm not sure there is any conspiracy. Jesús is still training normally. 1 don't think he's any threat to anyone. I just wish you could do something to keep that guy away from our training camp."

J. Edgar Hoover looks up at heaven blocked from his view by the off-white ceiling of the Sherwood Hotel. "If only I could round up every Communist and ship him off to Russia; ah; if I could do that, young man, then I could spend my days on the beaches and golf courses. I could retire and enjoy the fruits of my long labor in behalf of this nation. We have in this democracy a mixed blessing. The ones that want to kill you, throw your body to the dogs and take everything you have—they've got the same rights you do. They can go around and do anything they want to. Until there's evidence all we can do is watch. And now we're watching your fighter. And you."

"But what can Jesús do? He's harmless even if he is a Communist."

"Do you have any idea what a world champion is worth to the International Communist movement? Probably as much as the atom bomb. Do you know what people in Africa and Asia think of when they think about us? They think about our cars and hot dogs and our movie stars and our champions. Do you know that Cassius Clay three years ago turned the Black Muslims

95

from a bunch of freaky Chicago Negroes into a world-wide movement? He did it with one sentence in the middle of the ring after he knocked out Liston. Now you hardly ever meet an Otis or a Washington. They're all Muhameds. Du Bois couldn't do it, and Malcolm X couldn't do it, and Martin Luther King can't do it either. But that cocky rascal Cassius Clay, he did it.

"Now suppose that in the middle of World War II, Joe Louis had declared himself a Nazi. What would have happened to our morale then? Thank God we had a patriotic champion when we really needed him. And Ali, for all the harm he's doing, he might as well be a Communist. How would it look all over the world if our heavyweight champion is a Black Muslim and our middleweight champ a card-carrying Communist? How does this make our generals and our congressmen look in the eyes of the world?"

The Director of the FBI looks straight at me. "I'm not blaming you for anything, young man. As far as I'm concerned the draft-card business can be forgotten. A few crazy kids are nothing compared to a Marxist champion.

"You know," he says, "the FBI is powerless to stop anyone from winning a fight. The gangsters can fix a fight whenever they want to. We've got evidence to prove it. But if your Jesús is as fast as he seems to be and if he can take a punch, there's not a thing the federal government can do to stop him. And if he pays his taxes, we can't get him later either."

I am awaiting Mr. Hoover's offer to become a spy. I remember *I Led Three Lives* when we first got our television set. It came on between Arthur Godfrey and wrestling. Herbert Philbrick fought the Communist conspiracy every week. Men like Salutatti plagued him from phone booths all over New York. To his own wife and children he never explained a thing. Years later his friends by watching TV realized why Philbrick spent so much time in pay phones.

Yes, Jesús, I am prepared to spy on you. I am prepared to seek out safe phones. I am prepared to casually eavesdrop whenever possible. I am prepared to look over your mail, although I don't think you have ever received a single letter. I am prepared to tell Hoover at what hour you have bowel movements, what you eat, and what you talk about. And I can do all this without feeling guilty, Jesús, because I don't think I am betraying you, because I think you are innocent, because I don't believe a few odd facts in the possession of the FBI can possibly do you any harm. In fact, Jesús, if I can do these few things I will feel relieved. If you can consort with important Communists and not worry about what this will do to me, why can't I tell Mr. Hoover a few things about you? You know that I would never compromise your career, your health, or your safety. Maybe it's idle for me to try to convince you that I meant no harm. The FBI was watching anyway; they knew before I told them. Salutatti knew they followed him; you knew you were being watched. Until that afternoon I was the only innocent one.

J. Edgar Hoover puts the files back in his briefcase. The three aides finish their drinks and button their jackets. They unplug the fans.

"Here is a phone number," Hoover says, handing me a business card. "Call us collect if you have any information."

"Do you want me to call at certain times?" I ask.

"No," he says, "it's a twenty-four-hour switchboard."

"But what should I look out for, sir?" I ask him. I still don't know what any of this is about. "What shall I try to do?"

"Try to be a good citizen," Mr. Hoover says, "as you were when you phoned us. Try to stand up for freedom and democracy whenever you can." He shakes my hand. "Some day," he says, "I'll see you at ringside. Apart from all the business aspects of this investigation, I'm a real fan."

9

With less trouble than Jesús had with Otis Leonard, this easily does Debby excel in art history. "I wrote a descriptive essay on the architecture of arenas," she says, "without ever having seen one. I wrote it based entirely on what you and Jesús told me and on some sketches of the Roman Forum that we studied in class. You know that nothing much has changed. The Romans did the best they could for comfortable seating. The passageways and aisles are about the same width and the Romans never had any pillars to block their vision."

What can I tell you, Debby, you who suffer for the Vietnamese and put off your own pleasures for the sake of homework and exams. What can you tell someone who studies economics and art history while the angels who have been planning my destiny for twenty-four years, these angels and I, sit around and wait to hear your test scores? Yet the angels don't really care about your grades. They want a good mother for Grandma's great-grandchild. After all, her guarantee of eternal bliss ought at least to be sure of a good Jewish upbringing. I want to ask you, Debby, while you tell me about Roman architecture and Keynesian economics, I want to ask you if maybe sometime in the future on Friday nights you'll light candles and cover your eyes and make those half-circle motions with your hands that Grandma makes as if she is trying to pull the flames toward her. I want to ask you if twenty years from now when the war is over and you're forty-one and looking at the slope of old age, I want to ask you what you'll be like then. Will you collect money for the March of Dimes and the UJA, and make sure that our children take their medicine on time and wear warm clothes in winter? When I'm not a manager and you're not a student and an activist, what will we be?

"You'll be like all people," the angels say, "you'll live in a nice house. You'll go to work in the morning and to bed at night. If you're lucky you'll earn enough money to have a big plaque with your name on it on the wall of a synagogue. After you're dead, they'll light up that name every year on the anniversary of your death."

"But in between that plaque and now, the in-between —my life—that's what I'm curious about."

"About that," say the angels, "there's nothing to be curious. Only silly people worry about that—people like Mrs. Epstein who go to psychiatrists because they've got money to burn. If you've got time to worry about your life, then you're not working hard enough."

The angels are right. When I went every morning at seven to Goldstein's We Buy Junk and Batteries, I didn't worry about my life. I worried about the price of lead and copper and about the transmission on the pickup. Now, in the luxury of a training camp, I sit here while Jesús works and I wonder about my life.

"Why didn't you wonder when your father died," the angels say, "and you were fourteen and had to decide whether to help your mother after school or try out for the high school baseball team?

"Big shot second baseman every afternoon from three to six throws a ball around while Frieda stays alone at the dirty yard, a small dog for protection and company. Why didn't you wonder then if getting three hits the entire season was reason enough to leave your own mother, a lonely widow, alone all spring?"

"He's like his father," Frieda says, never blaming me. "For sports he'll do anything. A boy has got to play. He's got sorrow enough; leave him alone now. Baseball is good for him."

Every time at bat I pressed to get a hit in memory of my father, who taught me years ago the level swing. On the Turner School field he hit fungos to me until I could go back on a fly ball at the crack of the bat and run right up to the edge of the brick building before I turned to spot the ball.

"For defense, you've got instincts," the coach says, "but at the plate there's trouble." The trouble is I want to please the memory of my Daddy. I want him who died before I ever played in an organization beyond Little League, I want him to know that I'm taking a level cut and watching the ball all the way. But I want that hit so much that I lunge at the ball, I strike out, I dribble ground balls to the left of the mound. No amount of hustle gets me on base. I do not hit my weight. "Three hits," I tell Momma, "in two and a half months."

"So what," she says, "you had fun." I let her think so to make her happy, but it was no fun, Momma, going up to the plate and seeing the disappointment of my own teammates. It was no fun batting ninth and hoping to be hit by a pitch—but not too hard—so I could get on base and use my speed. I wanted to hold back, to stay calm, to watch the ball the way Daddy taught me to, but when I was finally there, in the silence between the pitcher and the batter, there I lost all my concentration. The bat became just a heavy stick with tape on it. I could hear the umpire chewing gum. I swung before the ball left the pitcher's hand, stopped myself, swung again off balance and half mad in my anxiety to get on base. Jesús, if you were like that you would never last one round. No, we

101

are opposites. You, middleweight, you shine under pressure. The ring enlarges you the way I used to disappear in the batter's box.

And, Debby, I want you the way I have desired nothing since those base hits. I worry, too, about losing you by my lunging anxiety, my awkwardness. You walk to school among crowds the way Betty and Veronica did in the Archie comic books. You and your friends talk a lot about the terrible war, but I can see by the way you tease one another that your own lives are not as grim as you pretend. You try, Debby, to integrate me into the company of the undergraduates, but I am as ill at ease among them as if I were a Viet Cong. I can talk sports or a little politics too, if I have to, but really what I want when you have me there among your friends—I really want them all to go off to a rally and leave us alone together. When they leave, you stop smoking, you smile less, you notice how much I want you. Then, laughing, you tell me, "Ira, all you like to do is fuck and go to the movies." You try to tease me as if I'm one of the friends from your classes, but I don't know how to respond. I offer to learn other pleasures, dining out, the theater, opera, ballet, museums of all kinds.

"No," Debby says, "I know that you'd do a lot of things just to please me, but it's got to be spontaneous or it's no good. I don't want to train you to like going to the museum. If you don't respond to art, you just don't. I'm surprised you don't just because you're a sensitive person, but I'm not going to teach you. Someday, when you want to, when you're ready, you'll look at a painting or a piece of sculpture and see the world whole, right there before your eyes."

Not me, Debby. All I'll ever see is what Grandma calls a *getch*, an idol. To me, a museum is a Philistine temple right in downtown Detroit. When I first read

102

about Samson, the Detroit Art Museum was the very building I imagined him pulling down. Delilah stood there on Woodward Avenue watching the gray limestone crumble around her, regretting deceit, honoring, but too late, the long-haired Hebrew who liked only screwing and going to the movies.

The museums, the Masonic Temples, even some of the parks with their big, gray horsemen all remind me of Baal and Astarte. Just to be a Cub Scout I have to get Grandma's interpretation of whether I can go into the basement of the Catholic church where the meetings are held.

"Don't take off your hat," Grandma warns me. "Not if there are idols there. If you take off your hat, it's the same as bowing down to them."

"Don't be silly," Frieda and Abe tell me, "go to the meetings and do what everyone else does. There are other Jewish boys in the group. The den mother herself is a Hadassah lady." But when it comes down to it, Grandma, I keep my little blue cub scout beanie on. During "The Star Spangled Banner," during the silent prayer, during the pledge to the flag and the scout's salute my cap stays on. The Virgin Mary near the coat rack, the saints in the crevices are waiting for my hair to peek out.

"Good for you," Grandma says when I tell her, but after a few meetings I quit cub scouts. Week after week I cannot face the pressure of so many idols.

"This is the twentieth century," Debby reminds me, "when are you going to stop believing what your grandmother told you when you were six years old?"

At any time I'm ready, Debby. I'm ready to believe that I can take my hat off in church, ready to believe that Solomon is not a Hitler, ready to give up the evil eye, the angels, the Messiah carrying his shofar in a

103

silver case. I'm not only ready, maybe I already have given up. Am I not here at Solomon's resort, sculpting in the flesh of Jesús a career as pagan as any in old Rome?

"It's true," Debby says, "that you're involved in a business that is almost universally looked down upon. But I don't hold that against you because all of your intentions are good. I believe in intentions. That's why I don't trust political leaders. They all want power. What do you want?"

I want you, Debby, and a championship for Jesús. I want Momma and Grandma back in one house and Solomon far away counting his money. I want our child wearing his hat if he has to among the Freemasons and the Scouts. I want boxing to return to Detroit the way it was in the heyday of Joe Louis. I want a pennant for the Tigers. I want to hit .360 and watch myself swing the bat slow motion in an instructional film. I want my father back in the pickup giving me yellow leather mittens so that I can help him load batteries without getting acid on my hands. I want to know what our life will be like in twenty years and in forty and in sixty. And after that too.

"For the first time," the angels say, "he's talking a little like a Talmud *chochem*. He wants to live long and know things. Who doesn't? But it's not so easy. You've made your list, now go out and do 699 good deeds every day. Follow the ten commandments and all the customs down to their slightest nuance."

"No," I say, "I can't." It took all I had to keep my hat on. But I'll have good intentions. Debby believes this is enough.

The angels moan like the crowd when a hero strikes out. They span the dark green earth spying out Jewesses in the pampas of the Argentine, in the wild loneliness of Australia. In Kansas City at the Jewish Community

104

Center, beside the pools of exotic hotels in Miami Beach, at delicatessens in Mexico City, in every corner of the Holy Land itself—they seek out an alternate bride.

"No luck," say the angels.

"Destiny," says the would-be groom.

"I've got to study," says Debby, "maybe next week."

10

In your published memoirs, Jesús, I do not recognize you. Of course, I am hurt when you refer to your manager as "the tool of the FBI and the CIA, and the Judas Iscariot of the Antiwar Movement," but I think that all of the venom that is in that book has been put there by someone other than you. The ghost writer provided by your Soviet publisher managed to get in all the name calling. The real Jesús is hidden in that propaganda pamphlet. Only in one small section—when you relate your first conversation with Tom Hayden—only there do I hear Jesús uncensored by the Soviets. Let me quote briefly the one honest fragment of that document.

From the *Memoirs* of Jesús the Crab (pp. 48–51):

Tom Hayden, he says, "Crab, why are you letting them exploit you?"

I say, "Tom, what the hell. I spent a lot of hours whittling my fingernails in reform school. What the hell. Fight for money or fight for your life."

He says, "Man, join us. We're fighting to change the world."

I say, "Martinez he always said he is changing the world. Fucker got his dick shot off. This changed the world?" Hayden does not know that Marx shoots out my ass. He thinks I am one dumb Islander and he has got to tell me what is happening in D.C., in Nam, in what he calls Latin America. I say, "I want some good

106

fights in Detroit. I want knockdowns and big crowds and solid guarantees."

He says, "What about all that is going down in Nam. You want to associate yourself with all that?"

I say I am gunning to be champ, not president.

He says, "Same thing."

I say, "'You bring that crowd of marchers down to Motor City and you swell my gate, then I march with you."

He says, "If we swell your gate, that warmonger Solomon will get richer. Man, we are not paying taxes, we are not paying the phone company, we boycott the table grape. You expect us to pay admissions to a man who sells metals to General Dynamics and fabricated steel to Lockheed? You don't know the new radicals, my man, if you think we'd go to support a warmonger just to get a little publicity and a good man on our side. If you didn't want to be one with us," he says, "why did you come out here to the rallies, to the teach-ins? Why didn't you just stay in the gym and pack your nuts in hot towels?"

I say, "Hayden, I pack my nuts with your kind of Revolution. Where I come from we used to say, 'Stalin says, we do.'"

"Holy shit," Hayden says. "Where do you come from?"

"From the barrio," I say, "but I'm the stepson of Martinez, Stalin's honcho on Manhattan."

"You got credentials," Hayden says, "like nobody else in the Movement. But this makes you a liability. We are not Moscow-oriented. To us Moscow is as responsible as Washington. With us you would be more respectable as a Maoist."

I say, "Hayden, I left all that behind me. I come to the rallies to keep my finger in the pie. I look for new friends and girls."

"You're no idealist, Señor."

"I'm a middleweight."

"Well," he says, "see if we're there when on Wednes-

day night you step through the ropes with Kid Sangrilla. And I'll tell you this, Comrade, deck Kid
Sangrilla and we'll have every welfare mother in Wayne
County picketing your gym and Solomon's junkyard.
Kid Sangrilla's mother is one of us. She marches. She
organizes welfare protests. She says her son is mentally
off and should not be in the ring."

"The Boxing Commission says he is A-OK," I tell
him.

"The Boxing Commission is in Solomon's pocket,"
he says. "The whole city of Detroit is his handkerchief.
They'd like you to kill Sangrilla. Why not give his
mother a little more grief."

I say, "Sangrilla fought a draw with Chico Vejar,
beat Kenny Lane, Luther Rawlings, Carelia Valdez. He
has plenty of class and nobody can say there is a glass
jaw on that face."

"The man's talent is not in question," Hayden says.
"He has an IQ of seventy-six. He should be in a hospital not a boxing ring. He is also thirty-three years
old and wears corrective shoes. His mother has been
trying for years to keep him from fighting. He is out-
lawed in seventeen states. All I can tell you," Hayden
says, "is that if you fight him you are on the other side.
We've been with Mrs. Sangrilla on lots of welfare issues, we're not about to desert her when her only
son's welfare is at stake. This is like a little Vietnam
and you are the gunship, Comrade. Think about it.
Are you going to be as hard-hearted as Stalin? Look
what it got him. His own daughter hates the bastard."

"Hayden," I say, "I've got no love for capitalism and
its attendant vices, but a contract is a contract. Come
Wednesday night I'll be in the ring."

"Comrade," he says, "we are taking on Lyndon Johnson and the whole fucking army. We are not going to
shy away from a punk middleweight."

Hayden and I we start as adversaries, end as friends.

11

At the Salt Springs Resort, Jesús, you respond to the routine of the training camp. Your whole heart goes into your fists and your legs. Maybe it's the discipline George imposes or perhaps it is the secluded calm of Mt. Clemens that has turned you into such a dedicated pro. You who used to skip your run whenever possible and never do any timing, work on the light bag; you who ate Hershey bars and pizzas when I turned my back, you now train as if you have recognized your true vocation.

I see your dedication, Jesús, even though I am looking for something else. Openly and without apologizing I have searched your cabin for propaganda pamphlets, and in a moment of real paranoia I even checked the ring posts for hidden microphones. But Jesús the Communist, Jesús the watched is serene, dedicated, innocent of conspiracy, and a stranger to laziness. In his Mt. Clemens training camp, amid the uniformly aged resort guests the body of Jesús the Crab blossoms.

It is Grandma who gives me trouble. Of course, I have not anticipated that this would be easy. I've left every evening open so that while George and Jesús go over the details of footwork and practice incidental calisthenics, I am trying to introduce Grandma among the fifty-two current guests of the resort. The lounge is filled with the noise of complaint as the guests discuss each day the effects of the mineral water. Mrs. Rappaport's ulcer is better because they've upped the temperature two degrees. Mr. Berman's gout shows no improvement; he raises his swollen toe from a sheepskin slipper. Folded sections of the Detroit newspapers lie scattered on the floor. There are bridge games in progress and a color TV that nobody watches.

On our first evening Grandma walks in, eyes the room, and announces, "My daughter has become a harlot. Look at me," she says, "and see what can happen to anyone." She points to the rip in her dress signifying mourning. She has no tears, only anger. The guests, accustomed to chronic senility, go back to their conversations. I sit on a vinyl sofa, I hold Grandma's hands and convince her to leave the guests alone. "They are sick people, full of their own tsuris," I tell her. Grandma agrees to write out her case against Frieda so that it can be published and available forever throughout the Yiddish-speaking world. But to anyone who inquires about her complaints, Grandma will still tell the whole story. One of the guests asks me in the dining room if the fighter killed my mother.

"My fighter," I tell him truly, "is as gentle as the mineral baths. He punishes himself more than anyone else."

This, Jesús, I know is a fact. George Danton gives you little leisure. He wears a jump rope for a belt so that you'll never be without an extra three minutes of rope skipping. Before lunch and dinner he slaps at your bobbing, feinting head until you both break into a new sweat. Ten hours every night you sleep and two hours each afternoon. The rest is punishment. In this training camp I understand that the grace of your movements has not come from an easy life. Only someone accustomed to pain can embrace and endure what George puts you through.

When I trained you, I counted your pulse beat after

110

every run; I put ice packs on your face in case there were invisible bruises. I carried a jacket for you the way batboys trail a pitcher who gets on base. Just as Frieda made me take cod liver oil, so I spooned it down you every morning in case the eggs, juice, toast, and sausages were not quite enough for the kind of ferocity that had to grow within you.

But George Danton, your professional trainer, handles you as if you're a racing car out on a testing track. "Ten miles every morning," he decrees, "even before orange juice." Heavy with sleep, and sockless on these cold mornings, Jesús, you wind your way through the woods surrounding the coronary victims and other invalids of the Salt Springs Resort.

I eat breakfast and wait for you. I watch the guests enter the dining hall on stiff limbs and with hands pressing against aches at the small of the back. I listen to the complaints of the sleepless and the chronically ill. And while they take their bran flakes and prune juice, their hot oatmeal or their corn flakes, you race along their perimeter as if to mock the pain of their every step.

Still, they don't resent you, these old Jews of Mt. Clemens. They respond to you the way Grandma did— as if you are from a race superior in strength to the human but barbarous in your heart. They don't envy power that is directed solely at hitting another man. If you got up so early and ran so fast to distribute newspapers or to deliver milk and then came home to count your profits in front of a grateful wife, this they would understand. The profit from a sale not from a punch, this is the profit that makes men men.

Did you think of me as one of them, Jesús, when you wrote that I was a "capitalist lackey, a petit bourgeoisie, with the soul of a dry goods merchant"? Maybe I am that, Jesús, maybe in spite of all my efforts to think of your work as a job like any other, maybe I never quite

111

succeeded in making that grand leap that separates your body from your self. For George it is no problem. The fighter he trains is a machine that has to perform to a certain set of efficiency standards. When the training hours are over, he treats you as if you're not the person into whose hardened gut he has, scarcely an hour before, slammed an eight-pound leather ball. I never hit you with the medicine ball, never slapped at your face in the reflex exercise. It was hard enough to rub iodine into cuts.

And yet, I know that George is right. "When I smack the ball into his belly," George says, "I'm keeping him from puking his guts out when Kid Sangrilla unloads a right hook below his heart." Yes, George, you're right and so are the Marines and the Boy Scouts and everyone else who specializes in making men tough enough to brave the punches. But I still can't do it. "That's why Solomon hired a pro to do the training," George says. "Did you ever watch a horse trainer beat the shit out of one of those thoroughbreds? You haven't seen anything until you've seen that. Those horses run their hearts out in the Kentucky Derby because they know they'll get their leather hides whipped for ten hours if they don't. What I'm doing with Jesús is nothing. The real problem is one of those two-hundred-and-sixty-pound heavy-weights that you have to sweat down to two-twenty in a month without making him too weak to stand up. When they said, 'do you want this job?' all I asked was the man's weight. When they said 'middleweight,' I said, 'you've got yourself the best trainer in the land.' "

Yes, George, you know your business. Under your tutelage I can see Jesús flourish. For you he skips rope to a metronome, he sprints the final mile of his run, he tapes his ankles as tightly as his hands. You have made him see his body as an instrument. The mind of Jesús is elsewhere—on girls perhaps, or on some dark covenant of the Communist Party—but his fists and his footwork are all here, all in the ring, all dynamite and lightning. The sparring partners complain. Young blacks from Detroit, we pay them twenty dollars a day plus room and board to move around in the ring with a man who could cut their life short with one swing. "He hits too hard," all three say. George buys them padded vests, the kind that deflect bullets, and tells Jesús to punch as hard as he can to the ribs. "If he gets used to marshmallow punching now, he'll do it in a real fight too. Boxing is instinct, habit. You got to do it right all the time. I feel sorry for the sparring partners. I raise their salaries to thirty dollars a day, and let them use the leased Oldsmobile that Solomon has given us. They button their vests and stay.

About your own pain, Jesús, you are silent.

When you come in so thirsty from the roadwork, your leg muscles swollen with blue veins, your face a dull red from heat and exhaustion, when I see you this way I think, This is enough. This is all that the track stars go through. In a few minutes, the breath comes back and they're almost normal. For you, when the pain of the long run is over, when the muscles are relaxed, then you begin the real punishment. You drink a quart of the water and dextrose that George Danton makes up for you, you unlace the sneakers and lace up the black mid-calf fighting shoes.

It is only eight a.m. Your day is just beginning. For you there are still medicine balls to stomach, the fast bag for forty-five minutes, two three-round sparring matches. Your hands will be taped so tightly that I worry about your circulation. Your fine thin eyebrows George will coat with petroleum jelly for protection against cuts. You refuse the headgear while sparring and your curls

113

droop in sweat. You who do not cut easily are daily stained by blood, usually from the nose or lip of a sparring partner.

Grandma rarely watches you train. A few of the resort guests drift into the ring room, particularly when you spar, but largely, you are ignored at the Salt Springs Resort. In the casino amid the round tables and cane chairs, there George has constructed your training ring. The room has a capacity of two hundred. Since there are only fifty-two paying guests there is plenty of space for a ring. George has used the little stage to install a set of wall pulleys, the light and heavy bags. In fact, the new ring with its white canvas floor hardly upsets the decor of the room. At eight p.m., while Jesús readies himself for bed, the bingo caller enters the ring. From this majestic perch the voice of the caller reaches even the hard of hearing.

George Danton, who supervised the remodeling of the Casino, did his best to maintain the relaxed atmosphere of the room.

"What the hell," he says, "the old folks have paid to come here and soak their asses and get some good meals. I don't think we should get in their way any more than we have to."

After the first few days the guests pay no more attention to the sparring in the ring or the punching at the bag than they do the waiters clearing tables in the adjacent dining room. While gambling or *schmoozing* they drink the bottled seltzer water that until a few years ago you could buy in some Detroit supermarkets. Jesús likes the mineral water squirted into his face between rounds. "A hit, George," he says, as the trainer squirts from two feet away toward Jesús' open mouth.

I am happy, Jesús, that you and George are friendly and playful with each other. Now that we are so isolated I shouldn't be your only contact with the outside world.

A fighter needs company. He is all loneliness and concentration in the ring. When he crosses the ropes, he
needs to know that there are people who like him even if
his jab was a little slow. George and you are like puppies
cuffing one another, gesturing with your hands as you
discuss defensive maneuvers. You two are the profes-
sionals. I sit back at one of the dining tables and drink
the seltzer water that reminds me of Passover, when
Daddy used to buy Grandma the Mt. Clemens water to
help her digestion during a week of heavy meals and lots
of matzo.

"He likes it out here," George Danton reassures me.
"Every fighter likes training camp no matter what they
say. Everything else just gets in the way when there's
training on your mind. Here, it's all there is."

In the early afternoon, after a light but high-protein
lunch, Jesús tapers off. A little rope skipping and some
eye exercises that George says will help his reflexes, then
an hour or two at the almost deserted beach. On most
afternoons all four of us go. For Grandma I carry from
the resort a big umbrella that I stick into the sand to
shade her. There are hundreds of them in a shed, a
reminder of better days at Salt Springs. Jesús spreads
himself out on a big white towel emblazoned with a red
crab, and lets George give him a rubdown right there in
the sand.

"I break my fucking back doing it," George says,
"but what the hell, he don't like the trainer's table. I
won't force him because—who knows?—maybe there's
some good comes from lying in the warm sand." Jesús
dozes while George labors above him. Grandma sits in
the old-fashioned cotton beach chair that lowers into
four different positions. I like that chair and the umbrella too, so much heavier than the modern aluminum
and plastic ones but more comfortable. I lower my own
chair to three-quarters reclining Grandma won't move

115

from the first notch. She sits as straight as if she's expecting someone to honk the horn for her at any minute. Even at the beach she wears a dress long enough to cover her knees and elbows. Her concession to the heat is to open the top button and tie a handkerchief around her neck, not a big cowboy bandana like she wears on her head, but a tiny, flowered kerchief that covers the bones at the base of her neck but still lets some of the warm breeze down into her dark long dress.

Grandma takes a book with her but the glare bothers her. When she asks me to, I read aloud to her—slowly because my Yiddish reading is faulty, picked up from the *Forward* rather than from formal instruction. "Turkey talk," George Danton calls it when I start reading to her. Jesús dozes right through it, but George moves away to a spot near the trash barrel so he can concentrate on boxing and not get caught up in our "mumbo jumbo."

"Antesmeet," Grandma calls George because he complains when the waiter refuses to bring him milk with his hamburger at the Salt Springs dining room. The three waiters, Negroes well past retirement age, are so accustomed to the kosher rules that they scold him more than Grandma does.

"There is no way," George says, "that a Jew who eats like this can get the right amounts of protein. I don't believe that Barney Ross did it."

Jesús has never compained about the kosher diet that of necessity has become his. He eats all those east European delicacies, the matzo balls, the kugels, the chopped liver. Against George's wishes, he now and then has some pickled herring after his run. "That kind of eating will turn him into a rabbi and a tub of lard," George says. He weighs Jesús every morning and every night, but Jesús, no matter what he does or how he eats, stays at 159.

"I've seen this kind," George says, "steady all the way, then two days before the weigh-in they balloon out like women with false pregnancies. I'd rather have him at 156 ½—that would give us some leeway."

The books Grandma brings are yellow and so brittle that some of the pages break in my hands. They belonged to her husband Meyer, and they were all printed in Vilna or Prague or Grodna early in the century. The one I have been reading to her is an argument against anarchism written by a religious socialist long before the Russian Revolution. "What good will it do," he wonders in passionate Yiddish, "to explode the Czars only to release the mob and the Cossacks onto the Jews? Beware, little brother," he warns, "beware of your friends who tell you that they will be with you in the good days to come. For us there will never be good in this cursed land."

Grandma is not moved by any of the early socialist and Zionist rhetoric. She looks at the water, the sand, at Jesús peaceful on his towel and she says, "Nu, Meyer, I've lived to see this."

"Grandma," I tell her, "there's lots of people that pay a fortune to spend days like this. When the weather is this good, you couldn't do better even at Miami Beach."

"Miami Beach is for her," Grandma says. She never mentions Frieda's name, it is always "her." "Miami Beach is for the harlots and the gamblers."

I don't argue. The sun puts me into a stupor too. I think of Debby, studying for exams now, still not convinced that I should be living in seclusion with Grandma and Jesús.

Only once in the past month have I seen her. And even then we had to make love quickly because she had an SDS meeting and two quizzes the next day. Debby is an honor student; would the angels pick less for me, grandson of genuine Talmud *chochem*? She understands

117

too, what I am like, why I can't be as casual with her as the fraternity boys and the other campus people she knows.

"You don't have to be so nervous or so quick," she says, but I see her books piled on the desk, I hear her Baby Ben alarm ticking beside the water bed.

"I don't want to be in your way," I tell her.

"Lovers are never in each other's way."

She kisses me and goes to make instant coffee. Only when she says it do I fully realize that we are, in fact, lovers. The word has not come into my mind before. Probably I've repressed it for fear of the evil eye.

I lie on her water bed thinking about it. Debby studies. She runs the eraser tip of a pencil through her hair. She rocks a little, as if she is praying. She underlines with a yellow Hi-Liter. I watch the movements from behind. The underlining is a furious gesture of the elbow as if she is rowing a boat. She takes a study break every half hour. We roll around on the water bed.

I've tried to tell Grandma about Debby. I want to give her something to look forward to. I want to break the bond that vengeance has put on her mind. But she doesn't really listen to me very much. At the beach she stares at the water; in the dining room she will watch Jesús work out, and swat at flies with her cane. It is as if there is only so much zip between us, and now that I have a little it seems to be draining hers.

"That's crazy," Debby says, "why should you feel guilty because you're asserting yourself a little? She's old, Ira, her tiredness has nothing to do with you."

You're right, Debby, but even you, my love, as wonderful as you are, even with you it isn't the way I dreamed it would be, the way Grandma told me it would be.

"To get married," she said, "you have to say a good *Haftorah*. You have to be able to go into a shul, and when her father says to you, 'You can say a Haftorah?' you'll answer, 'of course,' and you'll do it so well that he'll be proud to have you for a son-in-law."

So I labored, Grandma, learning that segment from Isaiah for my Bar Mitzvah, but not the way other boys did for the presents only. No, Grandma, I studied and I sang, getting the notes just right, because even then at thirteen I was getting ready for proving myself. I was getting ready for the day when I would walk into a synagogue that glows like the ring at a main event. The other people would be introduced—minor dignitaries— while I bided my time at the rabbi's right, looking straight ahead, not even checking the words in the book, full of confidence. When I stepped forward and the cantor called my name out in Hebrew, "Ira, Son of Abraham," the fathers of eligible daughters all looked carefully at their books. They were going to check for errors. Fathers, after all, value their daughters. "This Ira, Son of Abraham, will have to be something very special," they are thinking. And the angels are warning me. "Don't blow it, Mr. Cocksure. You knew your Bar Mitzvah reading by heart for more than a year and still Mr. Turetsky said you made three mistakes. Mr. Cocksure will come in and smile at the crowd, look at the stained glass windows, and then forget how to sing the simplest note. It's happened lots of times."

"Not today," I sing out. And as I perform, my voice makes the old ladies put their handkerchiefs to their eyes. The chapter of Isaiah the Prophet that I sing to the ancient cadence causes the fathers in the audience to renew their belief. When I am finished they rouse themselves from wonder to shake my hand. Long life and strength they wish me, and then they lead their daughters down the aisle, one by one. Each girl dressed in bridal costume has been waiting who knows how long for someone to sing such a Haftorah. They all march to

119

"Here Comes the Bride." The fathers are proud, and promise rich dowries. The girls hidden behind veils promise even greater riches. One by one the blue-suited dads, the white-gowned girls, they line up like Miss America candidates.

And there I am, Ira on the stage amid rabbis, cantors, Torahs—the panoply of several thousand years all coinciding in this moment. The dads lead the girls down the aisle. Each father carries a wine glass for me to step on. We assemble beneath a quickly constructed *chuppa*. There are so many brides that you can hardly see me. Instead my voice, only thirteen and not breaking yet, my clear, high boyish voice resounds in my Haftorah over and over. "Enough," say the fathers, "say 'I do,' and break the wine glass." The girls hold their breaths and the white veils hang in all their stiffness.

"Grandma," I say, "pick me one. Let's start early on the great-grandchild. What's the damage? I won't quit school. I'll study twice as hard. Holy men in Europe were married at thirteen."

Yes, Debby, by heroics in the synagogue I once thought I would find love—by my ancient song and not by my young middleweight.

"You worry too much about all the details of everything," Debby says. "Save up your worries for the big things. With me it's the war and school. You're scattering your worries too much. Consolidate them. It gives you perspective."

It's true that while I lie here on your water bed I have no perspective. I wait only for the closing of your book. But back in Mt. Clemens I wonder what we'll do when the summer is over. Grandma asks me nothing. She has put herself completely in my hands. I wonder what we'll do when Salt Springs closes for the season. Will Solomon send us to train in the tropics, or will Jesús, Grandma, George, and I move back to our old house so

Frieda can try every day to win back her mother's love?

And what if Jesús loses even to Kid Sangrilla? I don't think it can happen, Jesús is too fast and powerful. But someday his legs will be heavy, his guard will drop, his mouthpiece will go flying across the canvas. Someday I'll be kneeling in the ring with smelling salts beneath his nose. What then for Jesús? If he has money it's one thing, but can I count on Solomon to make sure that a battered and senseless Jesús will never have to work the small town circuit?

"Ira," Debby says, "why can't you just relax? Enjoy the moment. I love you. Jesús loves you. Everything is going along smoothly enough." She says this one day when a UPI reporter in the *Detroit News* predicts that the war in iVetnam will be over in a few months. Johnson is just waiting for the elections, the reporter believes. Debby is ecstatic.

Instead, Johnson escalates and so do I. "If not now, when?" the rabbis ask. I ask Debby if when school is over she will join us. The fighter, the trainer, the grandmother, the manager, and now the bride—sharing a life and a career. I know that Jesús might resent this, but I am willing to risk it. I am counting on the fact that he will find plenty of girls for himself once he stops training. And if he marries too, there will be a happy six of us, always at ringside.

"I don't know about that," Debby says. "There's graduate school, and right now with the way things are in the world I don't know if I can just live my personal life as if it was all that mattered."

This is the age of communes. Debby's friends are banding together in groups much larger than our tiny tribe would be. They are living in old farmhouses or in villages. In eastern Michigan, near Mt. Clemens, there is a group of former students who come sometimes to use the mineral baths and pay the five-dollar one-day rate.

The Salt Springs guests who see nothing offensive about a gym in their casino can't stand the long-haired men coming to use the baths.

"*Schmutz*," say the waiters.

"Feh," say the guests.

They make their own sign and post it near the bathhouse. "Weekly and Season Guests Only."

I know that this commune style is the kind of life Debby thinks would be romantic and politically important. But with Grandma and Jesús I bring along baggage too much for those new people who desire only small children and home-grown vegetables.

"Let's leave it the way it is for now, Ira," she says, "let's not press things."

12

Because of the new arena and Kid Sangrilla's mother, the press covers Jesús' fight with Sangrilla the way only heavyweight championships are covered. The scheduled ten-round main event is nobody's concern but ours. There is only one TV camera inside the auditorium; there are four outside where the mob roams. Mrs. Estelle Sangrilla has organized the welfare mothers of Detroit. They are there with her, maybe five hundred angry young women. The black churches are represented, and about two hundred SDS white students have come by chartered bus from Ann Arbor. The welfare women carry signs that say "Boxing Is Out to Murder a Defective Child." The churchmen say boxing is part of the violence that makes Vietnam possible. The SDS people have signs enumerating Solomon's ties with the Defense Department. "The arena is a front for General Dynamics," Tom Hayden is yelling through a bullhorn. All this attention has drawn the biggest Detroit boxing crowd in decades. Solomon has sold all 12,000 seats. Only Billy Graham has previously sold out the arena. There are hundreds of police and special deputies encircling the crowd. Eldridge Cleaver is outside exhorting young black men to fight the oppressive white society instead of each other.

In the basement locker room, Jesús, George Danton

and I hear the noises from outside. Jesús is on the trainer's table where George is giving him a final quick rubdown. His taped hands lie at his sides. He is silent as a mummy, so relaxed that he seems asleep. Yesterday he weighed in at 158¼, but he has eaten three big meals and is already several pounds heavier. How I envy his ability to relax, to almost fall asleep in the midst of all this turmoil only a few minutes before his first televised main event.

For me it is not easy. Debby is out there—one of the picketers against me. I find myself the ally of Solomon, Hoover, big business, and imperialism. Just a few months ago I was part of the Movement, now my own colleagues are picketing outside my dressing room window.

"Can I help it," I tell Debby, "that Solomon owns the arena and the exclusive right to promote Jesús? Can I help it that Kid Sangrilla signed to fight us? The boxing commission and the health department say he's sane enough and strong enough to fight. This is Jesús' first big chance. It has nothing to do with politics." (I haven't told her about Hoover.)

"If you had any principles," she says, "you wouldn't let Jesús do this."

"Jesús wants to fight Sangrilla. I couldn't stop him if I wanted to. You should see the show he is putting on for the TV people. He loves to be interviewed."

She snaps her mouth shut and runs away from me. I want her more than the middleweight championship, more than an end to the war, but I stand there outside the main dining room of the resort and watch her run to her Volkswagen and drive away from me. This is the first time I have seen her in three weeks. Jesús, Hoover, and Grandma have kept me occupied in Mt. Clemens. Debby knows that I am heartbroken at my mother's marriage, she knows that this is Jesús' big chance, and still she wants me to stop it because her SDS friends don't like Solomon.

"I hate him more than they do," I tell her. "I grew up hating him. Grandma is in mourning because of him. If Kid Sangrilla's mother thinks he's making a fool of her son, how do you think I feel when he's taken my mother?"

"Oh, you poor Hamlet," she says, "get off your ass and do something. Disown your mother. Picket him."

"And what about Jesús?"

"Let him go with Solomon if he wants to; he's just an unreconstructed Stalinist."

I hear Tom Hayden in her voice. Her small dark features are pointed in anger. To kiss her would be acupuncture.

Grandma comes out to join us. She still carries her walking stick, but in Mt. Clemens there are only squirrels to swat. Her bald head is sweating beneath the red bandana. Her cuticles are painted in Mercurochrome which has dripped down her fingers like blood. In her old age, in her stooped arthritic slowness, Grandma still towers over Debby Silvers.

"*Sholom Aleichem,*" Grandma says.

"I admire you, Mrs. Weiner," Debby says. "You have the courage of your convictions. Your grandson is too weak-willed to do what he knows is right."

"Who's this cockroach?" Grandma asks me, "*Vas veel zee?*"

I tell her Debby's name. I want to tell her everything. I want her to know that in the loins of this cockroach lie her own hope for eternal life. I want Grandma to know that this is the one the angels have selected for me. But I can't say it in front of Debby, who hates me at this time and would hardly understand Grandma's superstition in her most generous moments. But Grandma has anticipated me.

125

"A board with a hole in it," she says. "Too skinny. And mean. Look at those eyes. I wouldn't give you a nickel for one like this."

"You won't have to," Debby says. She goes toward the path leading to the parking lot. I pursue her. Grandma spits and goes back to the dining room.

"She doesn't mean to be rude. It's just the way Grandma talks."

Jesús, loose and sweating in the midst of his ten-mile run, jogs past us. "He knows," Debby says, "I told him. I don't hide things." Jesús waves, throws a kiss toward Debby and disappears behind the elms. George Danton is following him on an English bicycle, and keeping track of his time and distance. The sun shines, birds sing, the air is clean.

"You're worse than a Hamlet," Debby says, "you're a Svengali. You start the whole terrible thing and then you just stand back and watch it happen."

"I don't even know what a Svengali is." She drives away without explaining.

I have tried all week to call Debby. She hangs up. Frieda called twice to warn me there would be trouble outside the arena, but not to worry, Solomon had plenty of armed guards whose job was to protect Jesús and me. Solomon wanted her to go to the fight. She refused. They were going to the Bahamas instead for the weekend. "Can you believe it," my mother says, "me going on a three-hour plane ride to only stay for two days?" Solomon has already taken her for a long weekend to Paris. In the summer they're going to Greece and Israel for two weeks. How can I disown her? Didn't she work hard all those years in the battery yard? Didn't she resist the temptations of such wealth for a decade? Debby, from her safe middle-class life cushioned by charge accounts and braces, doesn't know what it was like for Frieda to

126

ride around in an old pickup while the Hadassah ladies tooted the horns of their Thunderbirds at her. She doesn't know what it was like to spend day after day arguing with peddlers over a nickel or a dime more for each battery and then hoping that nobody would steal the new purchases before they could be broken and the lead sold. She doesn't know the smell of the hot plastic cases in the air, or the sting of the acid on your skin. For me, Solomon is spoiled forever. Grandma has done her job too well. But how can I blame my mother for giving in, for wanting at forty-eight to spend a weekend in Paris or the Bahamas instead of at "Goldstein's We Buy Junk and Batteries"? I only wonder how she had the stamina to wait all those years. If she had done it right away, right after Abe died, maybe I could have been overcome then by a few simple bribes—a baseball glove, a new bicycle, a skiing trip. With such a stepfather I might have gone to Harvard or Yale and known at twenty-four who Svengali was without having to look him up in the World Book that Abe bought for my eighth birthday. Yes, he bought it from a door-to-door salesman. Yes, he believed the sales pitch, and yes, he paid two dollars a week for three years. But I don't think he got a bad deal. He used to tell me, "We've got it all here, everything from A to Z." He ran his thumbnail along the hard spines. The noise of his finger across all those volumes is to me, even now, the sound of knowledge. I recall it when I am studying for an exam. I can see his hand stop at the M–N volume, open the red cover and look through those shiny pages for Napoleon, right across the column from Naples. The shining waters and the splendid Emperor.

We really used to study those books. He'd say, "Just close your eyes and pick a book." He'd spin me around so I didn't know where I was from A to Z, and then the first one I'd touch he would take out. While still blindfolded I'd open to a page and there we'd start. Goldfish, Geneva, pen, penis, Wolsey, working classes . . . I had an alphabetical education. I remember more of the things we read that way than anything I ever learned in school. And Abe, though he'd never finished high school, was a wonderful quizzer. He loved facts. "Who was the first soldier killed in the American Revolution? Who was the first Jewish Supreme Court Justice? Who holds the National League home-run record?" When I learned the answers to all of his stumpers, we went through the encyclopedia looking for new "hard-but-not-impossible questions." "Impossible is not fair," Abe taught me.

Impossible it must have been for those ten years for Frieda to even let herself imagine what it would be like to go to the Bahamas for a weekend or drive a Cadillac or have a charge account at Saks. And now that it had happened how she must regret those wasted years.

And Grandma, for whose ancient grudge she denied herself and me everything, now takes no pleasure in life except the compilation of the case against her daughter. She is writing it out. Every evening after she completes her prayers she sits down with her green-and-black fountain pen and begins in Yiddish to strengthen her case Her writing is bad since she can barely close her hand enough to hold the pen. She writes on unlined stationery with the name SALT SPRINGS RESORT at the top of each page.

"To the whole world," she writes. "Everyone should know what can happen in any family. Death you expect. Also pogroms, small meannesses from your friends, to be ignored by your grandchildren, arthritis—all this is normal. But live with a daughter forty-eight years. To think in her body runs the blood of one of the Almighty's true saints, dead before his time, too good for

128

this world. To think that at the age when people are getting ready for social security she runs away to sleep with Satan himself. To me she's dead, but other parents can learn from this . . ."

Grandma, Grandma, what can we learn. When you told me the Solomon stories, I thought of him as a big dark bearlike man who hid in alleys waiting for young girls. Why didn't you tell me, Grandma, how he wanted her for all those years? I was ten and asking all the usual questions before Abe told me he never saw Frieda until the day they were engaged. To Frieda, Grandma, to the daughter you now curse, the span that made me must seem like a long, unjust interruption in her life. Abe and I are accidents created by you. Solomon, who is next to Hitler, Grandma, maybe he deserved her all along.

I can imagine myself his real son. I am a little shorter, a little thinner. I wear a pinky ring and keep lots of bills in a silver money clip. I drive around in a convertible. Girls like Debby Silvers call me every day. So do stockbrokers. He and Momma are gone most of the time, on cruises. They bring me expensive presents from all over the world. Instead of Abe's World Book, Solomon has bought for his only son a complete library as big as the Junior Adult Room at the Bridge Street Branch where Frieda used to take me twice a week. And it's not just the money, Grandma, it feels good to have a real live Dad, even if he's gone a lot of the time.

Solomon, can you teach me to shoot pool the way Abe did? "Always think two shots in advance," Abe says, "and never let your cue ball rest in a corner." Behind the back or one-handed without a bridge, Abe can sink any shot on the table. People in the midst of games they are paying for stop to watch him. I am proud of my dad. I put the blue chalk on the tip of his cue stick; I make sure there is talcum powder for his hand.

129

With me he is patient, but I can't line my shots up like he does. After about two feet my vision falters. I can't see straight lines to the pocket like he does.

"Daddy," I ask him, "why can't we have our own pool table? I would practice all the time."

"Then you'd be so good that I wouldn't have a chance against you." Why didn't it ever bother you, Daddy, that you couldn't afford a table and had to take me to the YMCA in a bad neighborhood where it was hard to find a parking place?

Had Grandma let her marry Solomon I would be managing an empire now instead of a middleweight. I would own horses if I wanted sport, and I would have a billiard table in the den. "Think two shots in advance," you teach me, dead father, but how far in advance are you thinking when Grandma with her eyes swollen from two days of crying comes to your house with the rabbi? Are you thinking of me at that time, of your battery business, of your heart attack nineteen years into the future? No, you're thinking only of the dark-eyed, beautiful Frieda in the last row of the women's section of the synagogue looking so childlike beside her tall strong mother. You're not thinking beyond kissing her, beyond sleeping with her every night for nineteen years. You're not even thinking of me, who will grow up only half-fathered, half-educated, not even able to decide what he should do at the moment he and his fighter have been awaiting.

Outside the armory, another romance is beginning. Tom Hayden and Jane Fonda are meeting. She is in Detroit shooting a new movie and has come over to lend her sympathy to the protestors. She is still wearing heavy makeup and the 1920's costume of the film. Her cheeks are heavy with rouge, her voice is cracking from a day of takes in a crowd scene. In fact, what she has just left is only slightly more chaotic than the scene outside the

130

armory. Hayden recognizes her, calls her to the make-shift speaker's platform right above our locker room window.

"Hey, you can see right up her dress from here," George Danton says. Jesús comes off the trainer's table to join George at the window. Jesús raises his taped hands to his eyes so he can see better.

"I wish I could promise you her after you deck San-grilla," George says. Jesús smiles. We can barely pick out her voice, but she is talking to the crowd. Hayden raises her fist into the air as if he is the referee and she the new champion. The sequins of her flapper dress sparkle at us. Jesús, still smiling, taps on the window. Nobody can hear him. He climbs on a chair to unlock the window, opens it, and calls out to Hayden who is silent now awaiting the next angry speaker.

Hayden comes to the window. He has to get down on all fours to see into the locker room. "Stalin's boy," he says, "so you're going through with it after all. I thought you would. You belong with the Solomons of this world. You've always been their ally. We may not stop this one, but after tonight's publicity Kid Sangrilla will never get another fight."

"You think I keel him," Jesús says in a broader accent than I have ever heard him use.

"You might," Hayden says, "it wouldn't be out of character, would it?"

"C'mon down," Jesús says. "We negotiate. Bring the girl."

"Hold on," I say, "the semi-final has already started. In twenty minutes we've got to go upstairs."

"Save the girl for later," George Danton says. He is worried too. "Later. You can even do it here in the locker room, but you can't risk anything before a fight. Kid Sangrilla may be a dummy but that don't affect his right hook."

131

Hayden is already halfway through the window. The only way to enter is head first. Jesús catches him under the arms and pulls the tall, thin radical into the dressing room. Hayden looks around. He doesn't recognize me but he stood only a few feet away the night I burned my draft card. Jesús is still on the chair awaiting Jane Fonda. Her upper body slides through the small opening. She is a heavier bundle than Hayden. Jesús holds her in those taped hands then lowers her easily to the ground. He closes the window.

"Goddamn," George Danton says, "we got no business having these rabble-rousers in here. Why don't the two of you and all your buddies go raise hell with some politicians? Boxing's got enough trouble without this."

Jane Fonda shakes her long red-gold hair and pulls at it as if she caught some spider webs on her journey through the window.

"Jesus Christ it smells down here," she says. "I thought this was supposed to be such a fancy building."

"They didn't remodel the locker rooms," I say. "Down here it's the same gladiator pit it's always been."

"You know that and you still go along with this kind of exploitation," Hayden says to me. "You know how much money Solomon will make tonight?"

"I don't care," I say, "as long as Jesús gets his paycheck. It will be the first time he ever earned more than five hundred dollars."

Jane Fonda sits down on George's stool. She crosses her long legs and lights a cigaret.

"Not in here," George says, "too much carbon monoxide will get in Jesús' lungs. If it goes more than six rounds he could feel it."

"Fuck off," she says.

George looks around for support. "If you don't give a shit," he says to me, "then I don't either. For all I care he can come out for the opening bell with a hard-on.

132

What do you want to have, a whorehouse and a political meeting or a dressing room? A fighter should be concentrating in these last twenty minutes. He ought to be thinking nothing but Kid Sangrilla. He ought to close his eyes and see in his head Sangrilla moving sideways and snapping that jab. He ought to be thinking defense and footwork. Any man who goes into the ring with snatch on his mind is a full step-and-a-half slower. All the wrong involuntary nerves respond. You got to keep all those synapses and nerve endings taut, ready to go. He should be a rubber band from the waist up, putty from below. I've never even seen a woman allowed into a dressing room."

"Who's this nut?" Jane asks.

"Jesús' trainer, George Danton."

"Well listen, Mr. George Danton, do you know who I am?"

"I don't care if you're the Queen of Sheba and wipe your ass with pomegranates, you don't belong here now. Afterwards it's OK."

Jane Fonda drops cigaret ash on the linoleum. "Listen, buster," she says, "I don't know where you get your ideas, but I didn't come here to screw any middleweights. I've just spent eleven hours pretending I was a whore with gangrene during World War I. I'm tired. I need a cigaret. If you're so worried about your young man's lungs, get him a gas mask. We've got hundreds on the set, I'll send you one." She blows smoke rings at George. He kicks over the water bucket.

"Why did you want to talk to us?" Hayden says. "Do you want to change your mind and join the protest?"

"George is not wrong," Jesús says slowly. "I like the girl."

"Everybody likes her," Hayden says. "She's a movie star. She earns a lot of money because a million guys want to get in her pants."

Jane laughs. "Ten million," she says.

"If she comes across right now," Jesús says, "I call off the fight."

I don't even know what to say. I just sit there and let Hayden and Jesús carry on. I haven't hesitated to alienate the one genuine girl friend I've ever had, the hope for Grandma's eternity and my own happiness, her I've spurned so that Jesús can have his chance—and here he is ready to barter his future for a fast encounter with a movie star.

Hayden is not so stunned. "We don't operate that way," he says. "Maybe Stalin and Beria carried on little experiments like this, trading sexual favors for inconsequential political victories, but we don't exploit our women any more than we send mental defectives out to line the pockets of General Dynamics. If you've got to prove your manhood this way, Crab, then you're fascist to the core."

While Hayden talks, Jesús is looking straight at Jane Fonda. She has put out her cigaret. She stretches her arms and yawns. "Don't be so solemn about everything, Tom," she says.

"With her," Jesús says, "I would make the revolution." He walks to the stool and embraces her. Her dress makes a lot of noise. Jesús' hands are taped tightly. Only his fingertips can move. They stand in the middle of the dressing room oblivious to us.

"I knew it," George Danton says, "you can kiss the crown good-bye. I hope they both get the triple clap."

"Jane," Hayden says, "I appreciate the gesture but this won't do any good. We'll actually make our point better if the fight does go ahead. I don't think there's really any chance that he'll hurt Kid Sangrilla. I mean you can go ahead with him if you want to, it's none of my business, but it's not for the cause."

Jane raises her knee hard into Jesús' crotch. It cracks

loudly against his protective cup. Still, he bends in pain. Jane bends too, to rub her kneecap. Hayden takes her arm and leads her through the doorway. When he opens the door, I see Caluccio Salutatti on a folding chair at the end of the hallway, his sharkskin almost glowing in the dark.

"Jesús," I say, "I don't know what you want in this world, but I'm beginning to think it's not the championship."

He smiles at me. He rubs his crotch to make sure the pain is gone. "Keep your eyes on the right," he says. "I'll make them forget Kid Gavilan and Sugar Ray."

A messenger comes running down the corridor to tell us Jesús is about to be introduced. George puts the silk robe over his smooth shoulders and laces up the gloves. Jesús "Crab" Goldstein pounds his fists together. "Don't worry, boys," he says. He walks up the corridor into the gleaming arena where the thousands wait. Four spotlights pick us up. The ring is blindingly white. Bells are ringing. "Ass is not ideology," Jesús whispers in my ear, "I take him in three."

13

Later, when I find the notebook and some of the letters from Salutatti, a little of what happened makes sense, although I can hardly believe the Communist Party and the FBI put so much emphasis on one fighter. I suppose I'm still too naïve for politics. If six years later Agnew could sell out for a few thousand and Nixon for a few hundred thousand, then maybe everyone was right to make such a fuss about Jesús Goldstein's brief career in the summer of 1966.

Salutatti's aims are very straightforward. He wants you so that they can stage championship fights throughout eastern Europe. Belgrade, Warsaw, Prague, Sofia, even Moscow and Leningrad, he writes, would welcome an American champion. "It would be six times better than the Olympics," he says in one of his letters. "You could do more for the cause in a single year than your father Martinez did in his lifetime. The Puerto Rican children need someone to admire, not just a fighter but a political leader. You can become their Fidel. Train hard, and when the time comes we will be ready. Everyone is with you. The cold war is happening on the athletic fields, in the parliaments and in the universities. You, Jesús, are the soldier of the hour."

I don't remember seeing Salutatti again on the night of the Kid Sangrilla fight. In fact, though lots of people,

136

including three FBI agents, have interviewed me about that night, I almost feel as if I wasn't there.

The Jane Fonda episode only takes a few minutes but it puts me on another track. You, Jesús, you can do it. You can try to seduce a girl—even if you are only kidding—a few minutes before a televised prizefight. I believe that for you it is possible. You are so relaxed that you could sleep until you hear the ring announcer call your name. But I am disoriented. If J. Edgar Hoover brings out all my patriotism, then Jane Fonda brings out all my hero worship. Right here in our locker room, Jesús, we had a movie queen. Almost an equal of Marilyn Monroe. To you this doesn't mean anything. You try to screw her like you try Debby and maybe every other girl you meet. But, Jesús, to me a movie star is almost as holy as Hoover or the Pope. I am looking at Kid Sangrilla but I am thinking of Jane Fonda. Maybe it's because once I actually see the Kid, I understand why his mother and the welfare people are protesting. I want to stop it too, when I look across the ring at his unblinking blue-green eyes. He is a short, grotesquely well-built man. It looks like someone has sewn muscles along his arms and back almost haphazardly. From across the ring I can hear him snorting through his maimed nose. He is openly strong but anyone can see his unhealthiness. His eyebrows have grown together, his ears look as if they've been beaten against his skull. The ugly little man is smiling at us, and Jesús, dancing in our corner, throws him a kiss with both open gloves.

George Danton is still raving against women. He rubs Jesús' back under the robe. "Whole fucking place smells like perfume. They jazz up the armory and make it a French whorehouse. Joe Louis never even let a woman touch his glass of milk or press his clothes on the day of a fight."

We have to wait a long time in the ring because there

are so many celebrities to introduce. I am not listening to the names but how can I miss the tremendous cheer for J. Edgar Hoover, who moves easily through the ropes, shakes hands with Sangrilla and then very sincerely comes over to say, "Good luck, son" to Jesús. Not a wink to me, not a sign of suspicion toward Jesús.

"A real pro," I think. Jesús is laughing so hard that his mouthpiece falls out. "Everything is cute tonight, huh middleweight," George says. "Nookie is cute and the FBI is a riot and boy oh boy is it going to be hilarious when that ugly dummy slams you on your bony ass."

For me the rest is blurry. I remember only the atmosphere. The noise, the smell, the solemn look on Hoover's face as he climbed through the ropes, the way Diana Ross pulled at the top of her dress before she sang "The Star Spangled Banner." I remember the smooth feel of Jesús' skin, the weight of the water bucket, my own sweaty palms and nervous heart. I remember the precise timbre of the bell and the gray hairs sprouting from the nose of George Danton. After the first long look, I have no further impression of Kid Sangrilla. He is King Kong across the ring. I hear the uneven snort of his breath, heavy even before the fight has begun. I remember the lisping voice of the referee as he tells us briefly the rules of the Michigan Boxing Commission.

I think that for me the fight itself has forever melted into everything else that happened on that night. And yet, I stood at the northeast corner of the ring and watched Jesús trade blows with the Neanderthal man. I know that I was worried about Jesús, was proud of his speed and counter-punching—although none of the actual exchanges are now visible in my mind's eye as so much of the atmosphere still is.

And yet the voice of the arena manager in my ear in

the midst of round three, that I remember like my first glimpse of Debby.

"Maybe I shouldn't tell you this now," he is yelling directly into my head, "but they said to. Your grandma just had a stroke in Mt. Clemens. I've got a number you're supposed to call; it's in the office. You can get it after the fight."

I know that he walked down the steps and along the aisle and that I stood there, at least until the end of the round, but I was no longer seeing Jesús and Kid Sangrilla. I saw Grandma alone in that Mt. Clemens cabin, her Mercurochromed fingers gone stiff, her bald head pale and showing its large pores. In the last minute and a half that I spent at the apron of the ring I heard—in the midst of Solomon's new arena and the voices of twelve thousand fans, in all that uproar—I heard the sound of my Grandma's stiff body hitting the desk as she wrote. I heard the sages of Israel gathering above the ring to greet her soul, which was coming here for a quick good-bye to me, her "boychick," her ticket to eternity who had not had the zip to guarantee her an easy passage. The sages of Israel glowed in the spotlights, their beards fanned the prizefighters. At the bell I raced down the aisle toward the arena manager's office.

So, FBI, of course I am telling you the truth. When the tumult broke loose, I was in the office trying to reach Mrs. Wiseman—the lady with the stooped back and three sons who were specialists and had sent her to Mt. Clemens to relax. I was trying to reach Mrs. Wiseman to find out what hospital Grandma had been taken to, what doctor attended her, if she was conscious.

I didn't even smell the stink bombs until half the audience had left. Mrs. Wiseman beat the tear gas to my eyes by several minutes.

"She was just at her desk like always," Mrs. Wiseman

tells me, "writing I don't have to tell you what, when I hear this sound. You know through the Salt Springs resort walls you can hear a quiet burp, but this was a real rattling noise like throwing a chain against the wall. 'Bertha,' I yelled to her. I said it in Yiddish, 'Whatcha doin', what's all the noise about? You OK?' See, I was worried right away that the noise came from a person. It was that kind of noise, loud like a machine but still a person noise. So, when she didn't answer me and she didn't come to the door when I knocked, I got Billy with the passkey and we went in to find her spread out there on the desk. Her head was turned so sideways that I thought at first somebody had come in from behind and choked her to death.

" 'Artificial respiration,' I yelled to Billy, and laid her down and squeezed her sides and pulled her arms up while he called for the ambulance. I would have gone with her but my sons warned me, no excitement. I told the ambulance Mt. Sinai because they've got kosher meals there, but who knows where those two hoodlums took her. They picked her up like she was potatoes."

"Was she alive?" I am screaming into the phone. The noise is all around me, the crowd is running blindly for the exits. There are screams everywhere. Spilled Coke and beer flood the new carpets. I've looked dozens of times at the chaos on the videotape. The cameraman fled but the TV camera automatically recorded the effect of the stink bombs and the tear gas. The fighters continue long after the audience has turned its back. The crowd seems full of outlaws, for people tie handkerchiefs sloppily over their mouths. The security guards are also coughing helplessly. Even when the referee climbs through the ropes to run away, Jesús and Kid Sangrilla keep it up. Tears are streaming from Jesús' eyes as his body appears like an angel from behind the facade of smoke in the middle of the ring. As the smoke spreads, you see only a stray arm, the arch of a shoe, the top of a head. You can't tell whether it is Jesús or Kid Sangrilla. Finally, the videotape becomes all smoke. There is no sign of either fighter leaving the ring. Twenty minutes later when the firemen enter in their gas masks, the automatic camera shows the air clearing in the empty auditorium. It shows the handbags and jackets lying forgotten in the seats. It shows the nation's most elegant new arena as forlorn as a fresh widow. It does not show Jesús or Kid Sangrilla, and most important of all, it does not show J. Edgar Hoover.

It was hours before anyone even knew Hoover was gone. The morning papers treated the story lightly.

In 1966 a few stink bombs, some tear gas, and the disruption of a public event were nothing special. The early papers treated the disrupted fight as a funny story, one of the few instances of SDS levity. The national news even ran a segment of the videotape that showed the ring encased in smoke with a fragment of arm sticking out—Jesús' debut on network television.

Yes, for hours I guess it looked like a very funny story to the people who were following it. I wasn't. My eyes were still stinging from the tear gas when I reached Mt. Sinai hospital. I had put all thoughts of the fight out of my mind. I was sure that Hayden and Sangrilla's mother had carefully arranged to ruin Jesús' important match. I told myself all the way to the hospital that I would try to pick up the pieces when Grandma was better. But I suspected without being able to really think it, that Grandma was already dead.

It takes at least half an hour in the hospital to find out whether or not she is actually there. Then a cheerful nurse leads me to a hallway on the third floor, where they have put Grandma "temporarily, until we have a vacant room." Nobody can tell me how she is. When I see her, they don't have to. My powerful, opinionated

Grandma is lying there, open-eyed, clearly uncomfortable, and totally oblivious. Her face has an expression similar to Kid Sangrilla's. She cannot recognize me or even hear me. I want to tell her that she'll be okay, she'll be home in a few days and live yet to see that long-awaited great-grandchild, but I can't force myself to say anything. I move a chair against the stretcher, and hold her damp hand.

With only a couple of breaks for coffee I sit there with her all night. At two a.m. an intern tells me she might go at any second. At six-thirty they move her to a private room.

At seven o'clock, two FBI agents introduce themselves, close the door of the hospital room and tell me that Mr. Hoover is missing. I am too tired to care. I am thinking of calling Frieda in Nassau even though I know that Grandma wouldn't want me to. "You're a suspect," one of the FBI men says to me. "Where's your fighter?"

"I've been in this hospital all night. The last I saw he was in the ring waiting for round four. I don't know what went on in the armory. I was in the office trying to find out about Grandma when all the smoke hit. Jesús must be asleep. We have two rooms in the Book Cadillac Hotel in his name. If he's not there he and George might have gone back to Mt. Clemens. They must be wondering where I am."

"We've checked the Book Cadillac and we've checked Mt. Clemens," the FBI man says. "We've checked everywhere. You weren't too easy to locate either."

"That's not my fault."

"The fighter's missing and Mr. Hoover is missing. You can't say that's just a coincidence."

"I don't know anything. Look at my grandma. That's all that I'm worried about. Go ask Tom Hayden and the welfare mothers and the anti-Solomon protestors where Hoover is. I didn't throw the smoke bombs."

"They didn't either," he says. "C'mon with us."

"I'm not leaving my Grandma. She may die at any second."

They take me between them and hold my elbows. "Don't give us any trouble, buddy. There's not much to do for the old lady. We checked that too. Nobody can save her. But if we don't save Mr. Hoover I am personally going to castrate every pinko longhair in Wayne County."

"But I met Hoover. I gave him information."

"Maybe," they say as they pull me from room 340. "Maybe you helped to set him up for the kidnap."

"Who can kidnap the head of the FBI?"

"Communists," the agent says, "the international Communist conspiracy that all of you think is such a laugh. Hoover is missing, the middleweight is missing, and Caluccio Salutatti is missing. There's a lot of questions here and not much time. Your balls don't have a much better chance than your grandma's heart."

14

J. Edgar Hoover was not a big eater. Cold cereal in the morning, salad at noon, early dinner with wine. Nothing fancy, but always on schedule. His desk was clean as a mirror. He saved cigar bands in the upper right-hand corner of the top drawer of his desk. Fan mail was filed alphabetically and always answered. He hoped to eradicate crime but he was pledged to create order. Nothing could be mislaid in the world of Mr. Hoover. "Everything in its place and a place for everything," he used to tell new members of the staff.

Contrary to his popular image, Mr. Hoover was not tough, mean, or ruthless. He was easy to work for. He liked a clean, error-free typed page no matter what it said. He signed his name in small meticulous letters. He never used initials and he hated interoffice memos. The Depression and Prohibition converged to force his solid-looking jaw into the public eye. Given any choice Mr. Hoover would have preferred to manage a local insurance company office.

Jesús "Crab" Goldstein took a cigar from the inner pocket of Mr. Hoover's blue suit. He bit the top and gently spat the tobacco toward the G-man's foot. Mr. Hoover looked away, noticing that the middleweight discarded the band and the cellophane without first seeking a waste basket. Mr. Hoover felt nauseous. There was still tear gas in his lungs and in his eyes. Also, they were flying at a low altitude into a head wind.

"What are you going to do with me?" Mr. Hoover asked of the cocky cigar smoker.

Goldstein inhaled, coughed, shrugged his shoulders. He smiled. "Jesús the Crab, he only hurt people in the ring. You got no worries, bossman."

"I haven't worried since the depths of the Great Depression," Mr. Hoover answered. "I stopped worrying when the Dust Bowl grew fertile once more. I found my vocation and after that I let the criminal types do the worrying."

"Jesús the Crab is no criminal, bossman. This here's just good fun. You see pretty soon. In politics there is lots of joking around."

"Kidnapping is no joke, son, not in any country. And doing what you did to that arena, that too was a criminal offense—not to speak of the moral outrage. You made a fool out of one of God's unfortunates tonight. Kid Sangrilla needed to be treated like an equal. You robbed him of what may well be his last fight."

"This business is more important than boxing. You wait. Caluccio, he'll explain it to you."

"Son," Mr. Hoover said, "I've heard the Communist line in many a tongue. We monitor east European radio. I've got your slogans coming out of my ears. I came to see a good fight tonight, there was nothing political. Hell, G-men have to relax too. And you know I can't really relax while you're blowing cigar smoke and pointing a gun at me."

Jesús put away his pistol and crushed the cigar beneath his sleeve. "Sorry, bossman. The gun is not loaded. Caluccio just told me to keep an eye on you. I guess a ranking middleweight don't need a gun to watch an old man."

"After tonight, son, you'll never be ranked again.

145

You'll be scratched from the pages of the *Ring*, obliterated from any WBA-sanctioned events; you'll have to get your bouts behind the Iron Curtain." Mr. Hoover looked wistfully into the clear brown eyes of the Puerto Rican middleweight. "You know, son, it didn't have to turn out this way. You had a great chance to outrun your past. I read criminals like they're comic books. They can't look me in the eye. I walk past a line-up and point out the man every time. We've tried it in D.C., just to test me out. The local police can't believe it. It is uncanny. But what about those forked sticks that point toward the ground when there's water? They're uncanny too. I believe in the unknown. And I am not afraid. Criminals are afraid. They can't look into the eyes of J. Edgar Hoover. You're not a criminal, son. I'm sorry they led you astray. Someday you'll appreciate this country and the opportunity you threw away."

Jesús laughs, "Bossman, Jesús the Crab did not throw away nothin'. We just picked up guaranteed money in the bank and the big thing, the champeenship."

The small plane dips in the wind. The middleweight stumbles against the legs of J. Edgar Hoover. The FBI director helps the young fighter to regain his balance. The sun is rising. Beneath them the red clay of Georgia is moving toward the Florida swamps.

"There is nothing like being in a plane at dawn," Hoover says. "Even under these conditions I can't look at it without being touched by the splendor of nature."

"Yeh, it's something all right," Jesús says. "You know, Hoover, you ain't much like what I thought you would be."

"My fate," answers the director. "Nobody expects anything but a square jaw and a forty-five cradled near my ribs. I haven't even carried a gun in twenty years. You saw that when you frisked me. Criminals expect me

146

to be like them, you expected me to be worse than you are."

"That's right."

"My boys will turn the world sideways until they find me. You may kill me, but you won't be able to hide me away. You know that, don't you?"

"Bossman, Jesús the Crab ain't gonna hurt you. You take it easy, in a few hours we'll be in Caracas."

"So that's where you're taking me."

"Maybe there, maybe Montevideo. Caluccio's not sure himself."

"Why are you spiriting me so far south?"

"Caluccio's got friends there. It's too hard to hide you in Detroit or Chicago."

J. Edgar Hoover leans back against the hard cushions of the Piper airplane. He has not addressed any questions to Caluccio Salutatti whom he knows to be a Communist, a criminal, and the organizer of his kidnapping. Nor has he taken any notice of the pilot. The fighter is still wearing his trunks, though the gloves and the tape have been removed from his hands. Mr. Hoover is not sure who pulled him out of the smoky arena. He thought it was his own men. Coughing and choking, he followed someone blindly to a car and ended up at a small airport. The fighter and Salutatti awaited him there carrying guns. Now he was on his way to Venezuela.

I've had too long and glorious a career, Hoover thinks, to end it kidnapped by a punk fighter and an over-the-hill Communist. Still, the world doesn't give too many choices. Kennedy didn't know what was awaiting him in Dallas. Lincoln went to see a play.

Just in case he is about to die, Hoover lets his mind toss images of his entire life before him. He sees the lady in the red dress telling a group of them in the Chicago office that John Dillinger is in the Biograph Theatre

147

watching a double feature. Two of the boys goose her. The dress is very, very red. "Listen, hombres," she says, "after being John Dillinger's girl, I could take on a herd of elephants. Many a night he has threatened to shoot off my nipples. Life has not been a cakewalk. Still, no matter what you are thinking, it is no easy decision to rat on him. Even a bastard like that expects loyalty." The boys fondle her some more then get into the Chevy and head for the Biograph Theatre. They do not believe her. Too many times they have staked out the supposed lair of a famous criminal only to find themselves playing peeping tom to innocent folk.

Joe Allen drives. Bernie and Slim are in the front too. Hoover sits alone with the lady in red. The back seat of the Chevy is itchy, hard, very similar to the feel and texture of the seat he is now occupying. The lady sobs quietly into a white handkerchief. She is a small, well-muscled woman of Hungarian lineage, twenty-four years old. She has broad lips. She is no criminal. She leans against Mr. Hoover as if to ask comfort for her tears. "Grab her ass, J.," Joe Allen says. He can see them through the rear-view mirror.

"Keep your eyes on the road, Joe, in a few minutes you may have to face down a killer."

"Looks like you'll be facing down a beaver." The boys all laugh. Prohibition, with its long workdays, still brought a lot of laughs. Agents worked closely with each other. It was romantic to capture criminals. People really went to the post office to look at the "wanted" posters. Kids knew the vital statistics of famous criminals the way they now know football players.

Leaning against his blue suit, depositing flecks of tear and dandruff, she didn't seem to Mr. Hoover to be the girl friend of Public Enemy Number One. He saw someone led astray by the glamor of the illicit. He saw innocence shrouded by villainy. He saw a person falsely clad in a garish red dress.

"I'm from Indiana too," Hoover says, remembering her background file card. "It's for people like you that I want the world to be clean." She leans closer, dabs at a few more tears.

"Dillinger deserves to be put away forever," she says. "I hope it's you guys who do it. You're nice." The boys in the front seat are snickering.

A few minutes later they are at the Biograph Theatre and Joe Allen is dead. So is Dillinger. It happens before Hoover and the lady in red even make it out of the back seat. She is putting on lipstick; Hoover waits to hold the door open for her. They are planning to let her wait in the drugstore across the street. Hoover feels for his steel gun. She pulls at her silk hose. Dillinger, bored by the second feature, is on his way out. There are popcorn hulls on his trousers. The boys recognize him. He sees the sun reflect off their guns. He opens up. So do they. Hoover pushes the lady onto the seat, protecting her with his body. Her lips move against his neck. In ten minutes the photographers are everywhere. A routine afternoon becomes the beginning of a legend.

A few days after the coroner's hearing, the lady in red calls him. She is lonesome. Her friends, though knowing what a bad man she had, think her untrustworthy. She wants to talk to Mr. Hoover about a possible career in public service.

In the same black Chevy, he takes her for a ride. They go along Lakeshore Boulevard. She reminisces about her days in crime. "Once you like a fellow enough, you just start to think of it as his job. I even told some of my friends that my guy was a travelling salesman and we were gonna get married when he had a steady territory. Imagine that."

Mr. Hoover is persistently drawn to innocence. Had they met under more conventional circumstances he could go for this blonde, now clothed in drab blue as if to compensate for the dress that brought her notoriety. In the pantheon of women he has known she stays near the top—perhaps because the Dillinger case put the FBI in the limelight, perhaps for a more personal reason. Perhaps he is mistaken that night to look away when she says, "I want someone steady, like other girls have. I could make him happy." Hoover looks at her and sees a generation of girls gone wrong—hair bobbing, sequined dresses, white slavery, convertible cars. He looks at her and sees real beauty hung openly like a side of beef in a cooler. He looks at her and thinks of what it might be like to have a little bungalow in Oak Park, a couple of kids, a nine-to-five job with no travel.

"There will always be wrongdoing," she says. "I think that if we just keep our distance from it—as I swear I will from now on—then maybe that's enough. I mean, you could have a different career, couldn't you?"

He knows the moment she asks that his answer will be a turning point. Like Achilles, J. Edgar Hoover sees his options as the choice between a happy life or one given to the pursuit of perfection. When she walks up the steps of her apartment building and he stands at the outside door listening to the click of her high heels, he understands that his is a destiny plucked from the company of women.

"I chose," he announces over the hum of the engines. "I chose to fight and combat all attacks on innocence. Whether by individuals or by governments."

He opens his eyes.

"You're still dreaming, *Federale*," Caluccio Salutatti says. "Your eyes are open but you're dreaming about combating somebody. Your combating days are over. We've got a nice little rest home in Caracas for you. It's got lots of room and green grass and fresh air. The perfect spot for an FBI gringo."

"You're not scaring me, Salutatti. I know you like a brother. We've tailed you since 1947. I know who we're going to Caracas to meet. I know the street address, even the time of meeting. I know the code words you'll use and what your brother-in-law in Pittsburgh will say when he hears about this."

Salutatti lights a cigaret. "Mr. FBI, you think you know it all, don't you? You think everyone's going to roll over and give up because J. Edgar Hoover has memorized a few facts. Well, buddy, your goose is cooked. I hope you're a smart enough cop to know that.

"I've waited a lot of years for this, Hoover. You can't know what it's like to be followed for twenty years. Just to torture you I'm going to have you tailed for a few weeks so you'll know what it's like to have no privacy. You'll just go ahead and be a tourist, and we'll see you every time you take a leak."

Hoover looks the Communist in the eye. "Do what you want, Salutatti, I figured to retire anyway in a year or two. History has already had its say about J. Edgar Hoover. You got a lot less than you think by nabbing me. And you cost your boy here the chance to get a shot at the championship. That could have been a bigger propaganda boost than kidnapping an old crime fighter."

"Mr. J. Edgar Hoover, you didn't tail me close enough, I guess. We just insured Jesús the biggest fight of all time. We can fuck *Ring* magazine and the Madison Square Garden and all that capitalist junk. We're going to have a fight free and open to all the people of the world. There will be no hundred-dollar ringside seats, no fancy ladies in fur coats, no five-million-dollar gate. This fight will belong to the people; and you, Señor, you will be the fattest purse of the twentieth century."

"You see, Hoover," the Crab says, "Caluccio planned

151

all this with my career in mind. The fight of the century; we're gonna have it in Caracas."

"Hush, Kid," Salutatti says. "We don't need to give anything away. Who knows how they've got him wired."

By early afternoon, after a long refueling stop in Orlando, they are flying over Cuba. Just in case there is trouble in Florida, they hide Hoover under an Indian blanket while fueling. They give him a salami sandwich and a beer. Nobody questions them in Orlando. As they fly over Cuba, Salutatti and Jesús sing the hymn to the liberation of the land. Hoover joins them. "I know that too," he says, "and every other Communist national anthem. I know that totalitarian governments always have songs and flags galore but rarely a national flower or a symbol like our eagle or Uncle Sam. We have a course at the FBI Academy on the psychology of the liberation movements. We spend three months on Cuba."

Salutatti laughs, "You could spend your life on Cuba without understanding what is going on." He pulls the shade. "Let's take a nap. We got two hours until we stop again in Honduras. From there I'll call Fidel. If we went right to Cuba, it would make him look bad. You, Mr. Hoover," he says, "you can relax too. We're out of the U.S.A. You can be a regular tourist now." He reaches for Hoover's wallet, takes out the badge, holds it up to the light as if it's a jewel. "I'll keep it for you, Chief," he says, "until we get you home safe and sound."

15

I am jailed with the permission of President Johnson. No lawyer sees me, no charges are filed. "War powers act," an FBI agent tells me. "You can shove your constitutional rights until we find the boss."

I don't protest. Events and the exhaustion of the night in the hospital have been too much. I lie in my prison cot not asleep but too dazed to respond to the cacophony around me. They have me in a small cell adjacent to a business office in the Wayne County Sheriff's office. The FBI has virtually taken over the place. Local deputies lean on filing cabinets and drink Cokes. They are as puzzled as I am. I ask only that they keep me informed about Grandma. At eleven a.m. someone tells me that the hospital reports that she is stable. At noon they bring me a prison lunch. Nobody grills me. They just seem to want me to be close to them. Telephone tips from around the country come in every few minutes. FBI men dot a big map with the locations of the tips. Local police are dispatched to investigate each possibility.

Two voices are dominant. Ray Willis, the FBI's number two man, and Jerome Price, a Negro agent, head of the Detroit office. Willis's voice is gruff and heavy; the Negro sounds as musical as Harry Belafonte. On and off I sleep through the afternoon. Just before dinner I awaken. The map which I can see in the next room is full of dots on the west coast.

"How's my grandma?" I yell.

"Stable at four p.m.," comes the musical voice. "We didn't want to wake you. Are you feeling better now? Supper will be up in a few minutes." Price sounds so calm that I think maybe they have already found Hoover and are relaxing.

"No," he says when I ask, "it's just that we're settling in for a long grind. There's no point in panicking. That won't bring the chief back any sooner. We also feel a lot better about you. You look cleaner by the hour. Tonight you can have some company."

I wash, eat, and am wearing a clean prison shirt. How am I different from Trotsky, from the Purple Gang, from Eldridge Cleaver, whom I have recently read for the first time? My dreams of my heroic self would be coming true if only I were sitting in this prison as Samson sat among Philistines, repenting errors, waiting for one big chance to save his people. "Yes," I say when I ask myself if I would stay here forever to save the state of Israel. Yes, too, for the beleaguered Vietnamese, even the blacks of the South, but that's it. For the sake of Mr. Hoover I resent even one day taken from a not so busy life.

Grandma, alone, taking your last breaths. I hope if you awaken you'll know at least that you are in Mt. Sinai and not in one of those Catholic hospitals where the last thing a pious Jew might see is some pagan image. From that at least you are safe. My cell, too, is at least secular; if I should be persecuted, imprisoned, tortured, ruined in body and in mind, at least it will be as a good old American. This is not the kind of ghetto suffering your brother Esserkey knew. Where else but in America could a nice Jewish boy from a religious home even be suspected of masterminding the kidnapping of J. Edgar Hoover? Yes: I am here counting my blessings as Kate Smith used to tell us to. I am looking on the sunny side of things, absolutely certain that very decent black agent, Price, will make sure that I get a square deal. He will call Debby. She will come to me dressed in white. In a gesture of class Price will lock us together into the cell and then close that office door behind him.

"I've come to join you," she says, "for the sake of the times we're in, for the sake of your grandma who desires your offspring, for the sake of all the oppressed, all the forlorn." She pulls off her turtleneck shirt, her white linen skirt, her white anklets and tennis shoes. She stands before me with her blue-black eyes and square bangs looking like Veronica in the old Archie comic books. And I, I am as sexless as Jughead. I can't do it here on the narrow cot. I'm tired, also afraid that as a political prisoner I may meet my end among these FBI loyalists.

On one bare breast she wears a clenched-fist black power button, from her other bosom a golden silhouette of Chairman Mao dangles. "I am the Revolution," she says—not very dramatically because when I start to cry she quickly pulls off the emblems. "I was only trying to make you feel important. Ira, please, I know you're not a Communist; I know that you're innocent. I thought you might get a kick out of it. After all, you're famous now. You made the NBC news tonight and your picture is in all the papers."

"I don't want to be a Lee Harvey Oswald," I tell her. Already, I can imagine Frieda giving book-length interviews the way Oswald's mother has. She will tell everyone her Ira was innocent but nobody will believe her any more than I believe Oswald's mother. "I want an inquiry too," I tell her still sobbing. "I want a Warren Commission and a senate investigation. Even if they kill me I want everyone to know I was innocent."

"Ira," she says, hugging me in her naked arms. "Ira, nobody's going to kill you. See this belly now flat and hard against you, you've got to pump it up, make me big with seed, let the good times roll. Don't let being in jail get you down. Nowadays it's a mark of honor to be arrested. Only the uncommitted people, the businesss types stay safely at home. People like us are arrested all the time. My last year's roommate, Rhonna, was arrested four times for SDS stuff. Her father is a rich doctor. He bailed her out and all her friends too."

When I touch her pale arms, my thumbprints stain her with blue ink. "Did they hold a number underneath you," she asks, "and take your picture too?"

"Yes," I tell her, "I am among the legions of crime." The thumbprints cling like tattoos.

"Oh Ira, c'mon," she says. "I don't care if the FBI catches us." She lounges on the cot where I know that on days past murderers must have coughed and masturbated. I notice the thin lines around her elbow, the softness rising from her thighs. "Not in jail," I say. "Not now."

"It's romantic. We may never have another chance in prison." Fully clothed I sit beside her. "You know," Debby says, "we underestimated Jesús. I thought of him as rough and untutored, but with good instincts."

"To me, he was the first chance I ever had to really do something in the world," I say. "Even though it's all turning on me now, I'm still glad. Without this I would never have met you." We embrace again. It is a tender scene. The manager and the girl friend hugging on the prison cot; the fighter and J. Edgar Hoover in a lethal embrace somewhere else in the wide world.

"You'll get out of this somehow," Debby says. "I used to think innocent people were always redeemed, but that was before Vietnam. Still, I know they can't keep you for long without charges. I just hope Jesús hasn't killed Hoover. Do you really think he could kill someone?"

This has never occurred to me. In all the months, Jesús, I never found the killer instinct in your gloves. You were more like an artist. After you finished your work, you just wanted to clean up the mess. And your work was, after all, those fast gloves, those dancing feet. The punches are almost beside the point when the rest of you is so dazzling. I used to wonder if the opponents were as amazed by your style as I was, if half your successful punches might land only because the other man is hypnotized by the stealthy rhythm of your jab.

George Danton, who rarely praised you, told me once in private that he had never seen anyone, not even a bantamweight, with faster hands. "If he's not a champ," George said, "it'll be our fault. He's got everything."

But whose fault is it, George, that Jesús has now vanished after disrupting his first main event and is charged with kidnapping J. Edgar Hoover? Whose fault is it that the fast hands long for the Iron Curtain? In the long history of Communist sympathizers this is an entirely new chapter. Bomb secrets have been stolen, codes deciphered, penultimate secrets exchanged, but all subversively, all in those phone booths of *I Led Three Lives*. You, Jesús, brought Communism out in the open. A full half decade before the women and the gays you and your tiny minority stole the headlines. Unlike the Arab terrorists killing at random, you practice selection as carefully as the anarchists used to. Hoover, of course, is your best target. I wonder now if you were cunning enough to use me. Did you knowingly seduce me into phoning the FBI, and were you and the Italian actually spying on Hoover when he came to Mt. Clemens?

"What can they want Hoover for," Debby says. "If it was something to do with stopping the war, I would be proud to go to jail with you. But Jesús never seemed to care about the war. And that terrible Salutatti, the FBI says, is a Stalinist. I think this is just a criminal act, independent of politics. Maybe they just have an old score to settle with Hoover. He has been bothering Communists for a long time."

The outer door opens. Price, Willis, and four more men enter. Debby covers herself with her arms, but everything is still visible.

"It's okay, sweetie," Price says, "we ain't recording anything. We just came to watch. It gets pretty dull out there taking anonymous tips for eighteen hours straight. Just go ahead and do whatever you had in mind. Agents are supposed to watch." The men chuckle. Debby lowers her arms. "If the manager won't do it, any of us can replace him," Price says. "It's perfectly legal."

Some of this I am not dreaming. Agent Price is really here in my cell. His tie is loose. His smile is full of relief.

"Good news, Ira," he says, "the chief is safe and sound. We just heard from the embassy in Caracas. Venezuela doesn't want to get involved, but Castro came to the rescue. Your stepdad is going to be in charge of the negotiations. They'll all be in Cuba by tonight."

"When will I get out of here?"

"Not until I get the OK from D.C. But don't worry, if you're still here when the fight comes on, Jerome Price guarantees you a nineteen-inch color TV right in this cell. After all, Goldstein is your fighter and no matter what happens it is sure gonna be the greatest fight of the century."

158

16

In Nassau, Solomon is sunbathing at the private beach of the William and Mary Hotel. He sits in a striped canvas chair. Frieda alongside him, in a one-piece swimsuit complete with short skirt, is reading a novel by Isaac Bashevis Singer. "My mother came from this world," she says, "to her it's not funny. How does Singer make funny stories out of suffering?"

"He does it to make a buck," Solomon says. "They all do." With Frieda beside him, Solomon forgets business. He smells the sun, the wind, the air. He stops chewing cigars and grinding his teeth. He is so relaxed that his tongue swims at the bottom of his mouth. This is the life I always wanted, he thinks. Nothing else matters. On the island there is no industry, no machinery and no noise of heavy equipment. He makes no deals, takes no calls, talks only to Frieda.

"Next year," he says, "I'm going to retire. Who needs more than we already have? We'll travel half the year and do *mitzvahs* the rest of the time. No kidding, Frieda, I'm ready to start being a good man. I'm almost sixty. It's time."

"You've always been good," she says, not looking up from her book.

"No," he says, "I've lied and cheated on weights. I have committed adultery too."

"Because you married a woman you didn't love. A lot of your errors, Solomon, blame on me. Our years apart, they were my error—at least since Abe died. I should have come to you after the first year."

Solomon remembers: In his mind the decades spew forth profits. World War II made everything possible. His small bales mushroomed. For the war effort he bought waste paper, inner tubes, burlap. There was no waste. Everything turned to profits. His three trucks moved through Pennsylvania. People trusted Solomon's broad, honest face. He knew how to talk to rural folks, old mechanics who had saved up a few hundred radiators as a cushion against hard times, farmers with rusting useless threshers they were too lazy to cart away. Solomon convinced them all to sell their refuse. He sent portable torches along to cut the steel in the open fields, and forklifts to load it onto his trucks. He mechanized before he knew what the word meant. He paid high wages so the unions couldn't touch him. After the war, Solomon bought an arsenal at auction. He purchased tanks, jeeps, parts of mortars, machine guns, millions of rounds of ammunition. Anything that was steel, and broken, Solomon bid on. He flew to Guam to examine stockpiles, to San Francisco and New York for financing. For a few weeks in 1946 Solomon owned more military equipment than many nations in the world.

Most he sold without even touching, but a few hundred salvagable tanks and jeeps he moved to Pittsburgh. He rented acreage. He paid mechanics and body men to work on them in their spare time. On Sundays, when Solomon had nothing to do, he would drive to his acres of gory surplus vehicles and imagine that he was a general passing before troops. The air filled with cheers and the sound of saluting arms. At the reviewing stand, Frieda waited in a wide-brimmed hat with a veil. President Roosevelt and Arthur Vandenberg, the senator

160

from Michigan, had also flown in to congratulate him. The Hun was beneath their feet; the Jap, too, lay prostrate begging mercy.

"Solomon," FDR says, "they also serve who buy and reprocess scrap." Frieda is proud—and so much more beautiful than Eleanor Roosevelt.

"I did my duty, sir, as I saw it in these hard war years. Now I want to sell everything and go back to Detroit, which I've missed throughout the war. After all, I've still got family there."

The president understands. Senator Vandenberg is happy to have him back in the area of the Great Lakes.

On the sale of the war vehicles to foreign governments and dealers, Solomon earns, in 1946, more than a million dollars. He comes back to Detroit hoping to find Frieda.

A black bellhop runs down the beach toward the couple. "Mr. Solomon," he yells, "there's a very important message for you. An emergency. It's from the secretary of state of your great republic."

Thus Solomon, a longtime broker of steel becomes a go-between of the flesh. He tells the secretary of state that Ira must surely be innocent, afraid of what Frieda will do when she hears her boychick is in jail. Solomon is not stunned by anything. He never liked J. Edgar Hoover and had not personally met Jesús. The fighter was one of his wedding gifts to Frieda. He would have bought her son much more to make him stay away, he would yet.

"The whole thing is crazy," he tells Secretary Rusk, "these are not Communists, they're madmen."

"I agree," Rusk says, "but for the time being we have to deal with them. They asked for you to negotiate. They want a legal contract. We've got to go along. Most of Washington would just as soon let them have Hoover and be done with it, but we've got to get him back. If people think we can't protect Hoover from the Communists, they'll be afraid to walk the streets. It's a matter of national pride.

"They want the fight in the Sports Palace in Havana. Castro is apparently in on it too. They want world-wide TV with the networks paying the going rate; no blackmail, they say, just entertainment. They won't charge admission. Anyway, as crazy as it is, we've got to give them what they want. It's all peanuts as long as we get Hoover back. Agree to anything they want. The National Security Council says they are no threat. Moscow is as astonished by the kidnapping as we are. Their man says it's okay with the Kremlin if we go in and shoot them all. But we want this to be as peaceful and as quick as possible. You know we've already had a lot of trouble with the Dominican Republic. The president doesn't want any new problems with Cuba. Really, it's a good thing that they asked for you as a negotiator. The president wanted to send Averill Harriman too, but it's just as well to leave as much as we can in private hands."

Solomon calls his office. His secretary tells him that Frieda's mother is in critical condition. Solomon is afraid to send her back, afraid that a deathbed request from the old lady will tear his Frieda from him once again.

"Make sure she's got the best doctors," he says, "and don't ever tell anyone that I knew about this. I'm not telling Frieda. She has to go to Cuba with me."

So, Momma, while I lie in the Wayne County Jail looking at the ceiling and worrying about Grandma, you and Solomon ply the diplomatic route. "How exciting," the Hadassah ladies will say. "Imagine meeting Castro and negotiating for the government." They will wonder what you are wearing as you step down from the special air force jet that the president has sent for your use.

Cuban soldiers line the runways. Red flags float in the breeze. You are proud of yourself, Momma, and not very worried about Mr. Hoover. Why should you be? What's the FBI chief to Frieda Goldstein? He's out risking his neck every day against killers. Sometimes you just have to ransom him. It's like in business. Sometimes you just have to bribe the Castros of this world if you want things to go smoothly. Frieda understands. What she wonders about is Jesús in the middle of the kidnapping.

From the beginning Frieda kept her distance from Jesús. Grandma prepared more meals for him than Frieda did, even carried them downstairs, since she didn't like him eating with us. Frieda in the four months that she had Jesús as our boarder hardly spoke to him. At night she showered, watched TV, talked to Grandma about business, and caught up on gossip with a few friends on the telephone. She had no interest in middleweights.

"Will they blame Ira for any of this?" she wants to know. "Will people blame him because Jesús became a criminal?"

"No," Solomon tells her. The gentle stepfather spares Momma knowledge of my imprisonment and Grandma's stroke. The gentle stepfather is accustomed to multimillion-dollar negotiations. Solomon feels honored to be representing America. On the plane he and Frieda drink wine sent to them as a gift by the president. "May you have mazel on your venture," signed, "Lyndon Johnson," is attached to the bottle of wine. Imagine, Momma, Lyndon Johnson wishing you luck, all the reporters waiting for news, and you worrying how you are going to talk to people in Cuba if they don't know English.

In the hands of Solomon lies the fate of J. Edgar

Hoover, and more. My future, too, lies in his thick grip, as does the future of progressive socialists throughout the world who hide for a few days fearful of reprisals for this daring act. The World Communist Press condemns Salutatti. "Piracy," *Pravda* says. "A stupid crime," from the French Party Press. The Chinese News Agency doesn't even mention the event.

"You're wrong," Salutatti cables Moscow. "Think what you will of me, but this act finally brings us back into the news. We have become as tame as salesmen," Salutatti cables. "Let us give the revolution one big boost. Jesús the Crab, Salutatti, and Hoover do not matter. Let the world wake up to the issues. I am proud. Lenin would be proud. Castro understands. Let the best man win. But for fifteen rounds or less, let the world know that there are still men fighting peacefully for our ideals, fighting the battle in the shops, in the parks, on the wide capitalist streets where it must be fought. Win or lose, Caluccio Salutatti gives his all for the Party."

"Too many years in America," Fidel tells him after reading the text, "too much emotionalism." He slaps the thick back of his comrade. "Still, Salutatti, you understand the dramatic moment. Moscow is too dull. If not for us Cubans, the Yankees would have already forgotten Communism. This will be a good fight?"

Fidel greets Solomon and Frieda at the Havana airport. The soldiers do not look very military. They squat or sit on the black asphalt. Fidel is wearing a white linen suit and a Panama hat.

"This is purely a business deal," the premier says. "I took off my uniform to make you understand this. Today, I am F. Castro, a promoter. I am not endorsing anything about this fight."

"I understand," Solomon says. They work out the contract.

Momma is awed by Solomon's businesslike attitude. He is not nervous. He speaks up to Castro, arguing for every advantage. He could have been president, she thinks, maybe he will be yet. He's only fifty-nine.

For Jesús and Salutatti, Fidel gets guaranteed immunity from prosecution world-wide. For Cuba he gets all the TV proceeds plus ownership of the videotape. For Hoover, Solomon negotiates unconditional release the moment the fight is concluded. In case of a draw, Hoover is still to be freed. But Fidel keeps an option for a second fight also to be held in Havana in case the fight is a draw.

Representing both the United States government and Ralph "Tiger" Williams, the middleweight champion, Solomon agrees to terms. My stepfather personally offers to pay Tiger Williams $150,000 for agreeing to participate and to risk his championship in such a spectacular fashion.

"Naw," says the Tiger. "I'll do it for my country. Give the money to the boys' clubs where I got my start."

Tiger Williams figures he will knock Jesús out in less than five. "That boy has never gone ten; he's two years away from an honest title fight. Tiger will show the Communists."

Salutatti is not worried. "Even if we lose, it's a victory. We'll have a hundred million Americans watching. *The Daily Worker* never sells more than a thousand copies. The Third World will understand."

Hoover has a comfortable room in what was once the Havana Hilton. Frieda and Solomon are just down the hall. Jesús and Salutatti are at the National Boxing Farm, training for their fight, which has been arranged for two weeks. Castro allows Hoover to take a call from the president. "Just pretend it's a two-week vacation," Johnson suggests. "Sit in the sun, enjoy the girls. If anvdy in Washington needs a vacation, it's you. Cuba sed to be a helluva spot," Johnson says, "girls, gambling, hotsy totsy music. You could get anything in Cuba. That sonofabitch Castro (yeah, get that, I know your men are listening), that sonofabitch has made Cuba as dull as Poland."

The president also calls Solomon. "I'm having a good time, Mr. President. My wife is with me. It's kind of a honeymoon."

Johnson asks Solomon's age.

"A second marriage."

"Well, when all this crapola is over and we get Hoover back where he belongs, you and the little lady can just hightail it down to the ranch to spend some time with Lady Bird and me. You hear that . . . you bring us Hoover back in one piece and you'll have a barbecue biggern what we clamp on the astronauts."

Frieda worries about the pressure on Solomon. In Havana he chews cigars that Americans would pay two dollars apiece for. He spits brown leaf around government offices. The Cubans are not looking for trouble, Solomon gets what he wants: the fight in two weeks rather than three, an American referee, the pre-fight physical just like in the States, eight-ounce gloves, the three-knockdown rule. Solomon argues everything. Overnight he becomes knowledgeable about the sport.

In the heat of the afternoon, while Cuban fight negotiators take the siesta, Solomon and Hoover stroll along the beach. Frieda stays in, afraid of too much afternoon sun.

"Being a hostage," Hoover says, "is not so bad." He laughs. The sand squirts beneath his bare feet. "This wouldn't be a bad life, would it? Good meals, walks in the afternoon, early to bed, nice climate year round, and no paperwork to clog your mind. I wonder how these Cubans keep track of anything. While I've been here I

166

haven't cared a bit about any state secrets, I have
once asked Castro what his ultimate plans are fc
Guantanamo, or snooped around the sugar crop. The
truth is we know everything important. What I've been
trying to find out is how these Cubans go about daily
life, especially in government—you know, statistics,
reports, memos, the whole thing."

"Nobody writes anything down," Solomon says. "I
haven't seen a pen on the island. They all carry little
pocket diaries when they talk to me. They open them to
check the calendar on the inside cover. I've negotiated
for three days and nobody has taken a note. I ask them
how they can guarantee anything. They say that only
capitalists worry about legalisms. Maybe they're right."

"Castro sure can talk," Hoover says. "We've got hundreds of hours on tape, but in person he's really something. If he ran for office in the States, he could
out-argue anybody in Congress."

They roll their trousers to the knee and let the warm
Caribbean surf foam around them.

"I had a pen pal in Cuba when I was a kid," Hoover
says. "Antonio Duran. We corresponded until I went to
college. We traded photographs. I always thought I
would meet him someday, but we lost touch. You know
how those things are. I tried to find him the first time I
came here, in the thirties. I located his mother in a slum.
She said he was a fisherman somewhere. She hadn't seen
him in years. She said he couldn't write English. I wonder who wrote me those long letters."

"Life is strange," Solomon says, "full of surprises.
I've made many a fortune and had bitter days in spite of
it. Now I represent my country and walk on the beach
with Mr. FBI. If you lived in Detroit, we could be
friends."

"When I retire," Hoover says, "I'll sure as hell move
out of Washington, D.C., fast. But Detroit is not my idea

e best place. Somewhere around here, down in the
s maybe."

While you talk, men, while I lie bored in my cell,
Grandma floats on the edges of her arteries. She, too, is
in the warmer climes. Her brothers and sisters surround
her. The challah is covered, her father's little silver wine
goblets are on the table. Everything is ready. Her husband Meyer comes, wearing his black robes. Learning
drips from his long fingers. Her father hugs the bride-
groom, each man's long curly sideburns caressing the
other's. She hides among her sisters, but, when Meyer
moves toward the table to say the blessing for the challah, it is her eye that he seeks among the chattering
women.

"Oh Tata," she thinks, "I'm too young for him. And
how can I talk to a man with such knowledge? What will
we say to each other when we're alone?"

"Women always know what to say," Tata tells her,
but she never learns. With Meyer through the years,
much is silence. In Odessa, in Detroit, on the boat,
everywhere Meyer thinks and Bertha walks beside him
sharing the silence. The sound of the little girl finally
brings her the company she wants. Such a child restores
the world. Even Meyer looks up from the Talmud for
her, holds her on his lap while he sips tea, and lets her
try to pull the sugar cube from between his teeth.

Yes, once little Frieda is born, Grandma's world turns
back to happiness and talk, and they make a decent
living in the bakery. Detroit is not Odessa, but she learns
to forget her brothers and sisters and sit by the cash
register making change in those tiny American coins.

The girl is like a leaf. She and Meyer so big, and
Frieda pale, thin, beautiful, holding the hand of her
mother and father on those wonderful Saturday after-

noon walks when people sat on their porches nodding good shabbas; and Bertha felt like a princess beside this silent man whom all Detroit respected and who, her father told her in Odessa, would one day wrestle in the next world with the souls of Maimonides and the Rambam.

Oh, Grandma, in the deep shade of your veins, in the shrinking hypothalamus, in the hardened synapses of your nerves, in all the fancy physiology that I learned in school—where now can I find you? Agent Price stands beside me. Every day he brings me to you like a present, so that for a half hour I can watch your facial muscles contort, your closed eyelids flutter, your hard breaths push the white sheets up. You exhale in a rhythmical whisper—like Snow White's dwarfs going off to work. Death is on the empty trays, in the intravenous bottle, on the dark face of the TV where I see myself reflected, another shadow passing. Oh, Grandma, in all this craziness I just want to lie down beside you now and snuggle up like I did on the nights when the thunder woke me, and listen to you tell me stories about hunchbacks in Odessa and people who slept on the stoves and your little brother Esserkey before Hitler killed him. For so many years we waited together for something to happen. We waited for the angels to pluck out my bride and bring her home for your approval and Momma's delight. We waited for the Messiah together, Moses incarnate, who would blow a jazzy shofar and bring us back all the dead—including first of all your Meyer and my own daddy and make us one big happy family forever after. Instead, Grandma, while the Messiah lingered I brought you a Puerto Rican middleweight and the FBI. And as for Frieda, would you let Moses blow the shofar for her even while she lives? Frieda, your little girl, is not even here, Grandma, to wait with us for the angel you didn't tell me about. For you, Grandma, I want the world to come to be full of pious Jews, and Christians who respect us for it, big meals, holidays, dresses with long sleeves, soft cooked, low-salt foods.

Price leaves us for a while when the nurse tells him to, and with me alone, Grandma, you are lucky enough to spend your final minutes. I shiver for both of us. I feel your soul move through the air as graceful as one of Jesús' jabs. The intravenous fluid drips into your bruised arm. The noise in the hallway is loud. Trays clatter, a nurse's aide compliments someone on a hairdo. You, who for days have been only a whistle, are now not even that. My hands are heavy on my knees. I do not go near you. I hold no mirror under your nose, offer no last kisses, no wails, no tears. When Agent Price returns, Debby is with him, clad in a charcoal gray dress like a Catholic schoolgirl.

"Oh, Ira," she says, holding me as tightly as people do in such scenes in the movies. "Oh, Ira. I love you. I'll help to make it easier for you, honest I will." Price has his head bowed. A nurse or two come in and feel around under the sheet. There is no panic. A cleaning lady enters prematurely to mop the floor.

"You were like her son," Debby says. "You can be proud of what you did for her at the end. We'll name our daughter after her, when all this is over." Debby kisses me and finally the tears come for Grandma, for the great confusion of Jesús and Frieda, and J. Edgar Hoover, and the Communists who popped up like flares in Grandma's long and lonely life.

It feels as if she is my child, this old lady who for days has been a shadow on the bed. One of her hands brushes the button that raises and lowers the bed, the other lies against the remote control TV selector. Her hands are still soft and fine. The interior veins that dried out did not affect those hands that guarded me from everything.

"Ira," Debby says, "for you the world is just beginning. For both of us."

"Call Frieda," I say, as nurses sweet and efficient move my Grandma to a less crowded place.

17

Jesús of the fast ankles, the bolo punch, the head feint; Jesús of the clawing jab, the blinding hook; Jesús Crab Goldstein, as you prepare for your moment in history, do you train as George Danton would want you to? Is there steady roadwork, medicine balls to the stomach, two three-round warm-ups before lunch and dinner, shadow boxing at bedtime? I would have made sure, Jesús, no matter what the circumstances, that you were ready. I would have sharpened reflexes, prepared a high-protein diet, kept the press at a distance. If ever you needed us, Jesús, if ever George Danton and Ira Goldstein, your trainer and your manager, should have been with you, it was in those two weeks of pre-fight training at the National Boxing Camp in Cuba. But who aside from a few diehard boxing fans really cared about the fight itself when there was J. Edgar Hoover, suspended above the ring in a hanging basket like a topless dancer. Even during the live action of the match the TV cameras zoom in on Hoover, who watches from what is actually a very good seat. He is keeping score and, as his score-card later demonstrates, he is a very honest and detached judge.

The crowd is yours, Jesús, the way no crowd has ever belonged to a performer. For them you are Judy Garland, Frank Sinatra, and Hitler, all rolled into one shining middleweight. There are banners, there are people outside who just want to be near you, and there is a love that transcends sport and politics within that arena. Jesús the Crab is their national anthem. You wear the single color of the revolution, while Hoover's basket is decorated in red, white, and blue—not in the simple regimental style of the flag but in blotchy colors painted in spurts and various geometric shapes. Although Jesús is dark brown and Tiger Williams sleek and black as a streamlined panther, red is the dominant color. Red banners, red flags, the blood-red ropes of the ring.

Your final gift, Jesús, is to have me flown here to be at ringside, your guest for the evening. Debby, too, you have invited. I am anxious but with her there are problems. Her father doesn't want her to go. He is astonished to learn how involved his little girl is with this conspiracy. "I thought she was just going to anti-war rallies," he says. It takes phone calls from Solomon in Cuba and from the assistant secretary of state for Latin American Affairs to convince Debby's father. President Johnson personally guarantees her safety, so does Castro. To their minds this is just a quirky request from Jesús. They don't want to antagonize him needlessly. The government can afford to send a plane for us.

Right from jail the agents take me to the airport. I have only been out of mourning for Grandma for a few days. I didn't have to go through the seven-day mourning period, only sons and daughters are held to that by Jewish law, but at the end I was all she had. And what difference did it make to me in prison? There I sat anyway on a low cot next to an uncovered toilet, bereft of entertainment, Momma my only company.

Yes, Momma came back for the funeral and spends her days in the cell with me, her nights in the cheap hotel across the street. This week she has been the old Frieda, untainted by Solomon's gaudy millions. Grief has reduced her. She wears no jewelry or makeup.

173

"Ira," she says, "what will I do? I can't walk into his house without seeing her everywhere. I didn't feel guilty while she was alive. I knew how crazy her hate was. But now from the grave she is getting me. The only place I am comfortable is here in jail with you. The hotel has too many mirrors." Frieda, having just returned from Cuba, doesn't want me to go either. At the airport she and Debby's father comfort one another.

Debby and I are alone in an Air Force DC-8. A young lieutenant is our steward. He serves drinks, offers us sandwiches and magazines. "We're the friendly skies too," he says. "I envy the two of you getting to see the fight. Any of us would give a month's salary for a ticket."

But according to the terms of the contract all tickets are free. Jesús wants to be the people's champion. The seats are distributed from the arena box office on a first-come basis. The ringsiders have waited seven days for their tickets. People guard their places in line with drawn knives. There have been six murders this week in separate incidents relating to the ticket line. The American press covers the brutality of the wait as if it is a battle zone. The ace reporters from Vietnam are here, making analogies for all they're worth.

They keep us two hours at that airport, and then we are taken directly to the arena—V.I.P.s from Detroit, Debby and I to the ringside. I am remembering, Jesús, the flow of your body beneath my fingers, your solid confidence buoying my shaky hands as I knead the flesh of your shoulders. You look as fearless here in Cuba with the whole world watching, as you were in the Motor City Auditorium when Otis Leonard stepped through the ropes and asked for his second to hold a Kleenex to his nose. Those red satin trunks emblazoned with the hammer and sickle become you, so does that goatee that I never let you grow for fear of skin infection. Salutatti does not worry about infection He

174

doesn't care about your future in the ring. It is all and everything, all tonight. The goatee has not made you resemble Lenin, but it does bring out the romance of your background, the myth of sun and carefree natives. The beads I would not have allowed either. You do not need such accompaniment to remind everyone that you represent the unrepresented.

Solomon fumes at ringside. "None of this was in the contract," he tells Howard Cosell who is covering the fight for American television, "none of this at all. Hoover is supposed to be at the airport, not here in a hanging basket. If they pull too many more shenanigans, we'll just ask Tiger Williams to get out of the ring and let the Marines rescue Mr. Hoover."

"That's what a lot of Americans would like to see happen," Howard Cosell says, "but here we are at the meeting ground of sport and politics, ladies and gentlemen, where in a few brief moments the game that is no longer a game will begin."

For me, Howard, it never was a game, nor a business either. For me it was a coming-out party, a manager's sweet-sixteen. I wonder if Grandma would have watched. Probably not, Jesús; probably she would have stayed in her cabin in Mt. Clemens, continuing the list of her complaints against Momma. As soon as I get back I will destroy Grandma's notebook. This fresh torture Frieda does not need.

Jesús is throwing kisses, leaning his torso far over the ropes. Those wild Cubans are grasping the air as if foul balls or hockey pucks are actually coming at them. They hug one another as the glance and the outstretched arm of Jesús move in their direction. Strong men, workers accustomed to whole days in the sun, swoon when Jesús raises his arms and the red robe falls like crushed velvet at his feet. This is the international moment and all 45,000 in the Sports Palace know it. Lenin was a light-

175

weight, Stalin a dark counterpuncher. The rest were a bunch of nameless contenders awaiting the time when a Jesús Goldstein would come forth from the cradle of the enemy in his crimson trunks, shed his robe, and let his brown body gleam before the eyes of the world. Jesús, I can see from ringside that this is not boxing. There is no concentration in your glance; your shoelaces are not even pulled tight. I hope that George Danton is not watching. But how can he not watch? Who in America is not tuned in? The networks are not selling any advertising: You are the news, Jesús—for the first time a prime-time live boxing match presented by the network news.

Jesús is dancing in the ring, throwing kisses to all sides. So loud is the roar of the fans that Howard Cosell's voice is inaudible. There is Jesús in the middle of the ring, in the middle of the world, being loved in high decibels. He laughs a long laugh and seems to scream his own affection back to the crowd. Only superhuman restraint keeps them from tearing down the ropes just to touch their hero. My middleweight, you have it all—at this moment the world is between your hands. Tiger Williams, the champ shadow boxing in the opposite corner, might as well be in Miami Beach sipping a cocktail. Nobody sees him, nobody cares that he is 84–2 with 66 knockouts. Nobody cares about his eleven brothers and sisters in Oakland, California; his deaf aunt; his background as a star of boys' clubs and later, golden gloves events. At this moment, Jesús, while the fans scream as you are presented to them—at this moment I forgive you. Not that you have harmed me very much, but I forgive you, Jesús, for not going the usual route with me at your side. I forgive you for not waiting two more years and two dozen ten-rounders for a chance at a man like Tiger Williams. I forgive you because, right now I see that you are more important than the championship. When the cameras zero in on J.

Edgar Hoover, I see no malice in his look either. He waves to the American people; he throws two kisses of his own. Even in his ridiculous basket Mr. Hoover hangs in the Cuban sky as a distinguished man. His blue suit is well pressed, his shoes shined. This is a great sportsman at an international event.

Jesús has refused all interviews. Tiger Williams, once he has thanked his family and the boys' clubs, has nothing more to say. "I'm a good boxer," he says, "check the record. The record is where it's at."

But you're wrong, Tiger. Momma's wedding and Grandma's death and my own love affair with Debby—from here, Tiger, I can tell you that the record does not speak for itself. You are just lucky, Tiger, to be uncomplicated by even a draw. For the rest of us the record is not even kept. Jesús has just jumped outside the record book. He is now like one of those great race horses parading past the grandstand on Derby day while princes and millionaires gaze at the beauty of his strength in the sunlight and know that all their accomplishments are small stuff compared to such an animal.

I forgive you, Jesús, because you are right. Mr. Hoover, sportsman that he is, forgives you because you are beautiful. All across America and throughout the free world, fans and people who have never seen a match are watching tonight to see you demolished by the quiet champion. America needs a big win tonight. If the fix was on, it would be worth millions. It would be a fix bigger than the Mafia could conceive. A fix to revive a whole country sick of Vietnam and roving teen-age radicals and dope and irreverence from all sides.

Momma beside her TV probably doesn't see your glory, Jesús. She is too worried about my future. "Who ever thought he could do such a thing?" she says to herself. Her only worry is Ira. But, Momma, everyone else who is watching knows that Ira doesn't matter right now. That brown, half-naked Puerto Rican has touched us with glory. The rest of our lives will be notable only because we knew him. His presence swells the arena. It can't go on much longer. The announcer has been trying for five minutes to quiet the crowd, but the Cubans will not stop cheering. Jesús, enjoy your moment. I, who love and forgive, I see what is coming.

Half mad from this single month in prison, I feel prophetic. I see the fight before it happens. I feel the fists of Tiger Williams here in the crowd more than you seem to in the glowing ring.

For the first two rounds you toy with Tiger Williams. In the clinches you blow in his ear; you caress his back like a lover. When you duck his powerful punches—any one of which could ruin you—you make no attempt to counterattack him. It is as if you are Fred Astaire, there only coincidentally in the ring with a fighter. It's as if some business apart from boxing has brought you there, so you dance through the motions almost embarrassed by this lunging black man flogging the air so near to your person.

A light sweat breaks over your body. On the color TV you gleam. The audience is quiet now. They realize more than you do, Jesús, what one of those punches could do to the side of your head or the space between your lungs. Tiger Williams is relentless. He is a patriot fighting for his country as well as a professional champion who knows his trade. There is fire and ice in him. For a decade he has been fighting obscure Latin Americans, a few Europeans, and an occasional American midwesterner. But until this night his reputation has been known only to a few serious fight fans. He has bled in the dark, a middleweight champion in an age dominated by team sports. Nothing can stop the mechanical onslaught of Tiger Williams. The crowd understands his power. Some of those punches will have to land on the smiling face as they already have begun to pound out a rhythm on the ribs.

J. Edgar Hoover in the hanging basket is never forgotten. One camera is always focused on him, as if for protection. His image is shown in the upper right-hand corner of the screen. It reminds us constantly that this is no ordinary athletic event. Hoover roots for Tiger Williams. In a quiet and dignified way he lifts his arms in pleasure when the Tiger attacks, lets his program drop to his knee when Jesús outmaneuvers the champ. But he does nothing histrionic. Hoover does not act as if his own life might be at stake. An experienced soldier of fortune, he gazes down at the battle beneath him, sips from his glass of white wine, and seems content to let Fortune have her way with him.

Hoover on this night, Jesús, Hoover is smarter than all of us. He hangs there calmly watching a fight. He is J. Edgar Hoover and what else is there to prove? The rest of us come out fighting at every bell. Faith in capitalism, genetics, zip—whatever it is that I lacked to become a moneyearning man of the world—that Hoover has in excess. He is tranquil above the swelling mass, quiet in the roar. He is the prize, the occasion of all this spectacle, and he stays calm as a Lake Michigan fisherman on a warm summer afternoon.

"It gives me the creeps," Debby says, "to see him so relaxed up there. I wish he would bang his fist and say he has to go to the bathroom or something."

Between the rounds Jesús does not sit in his corner. During the minute of rest, he courts his fans; he stands at mid-ring, tired and exposed, soaking in their approval. He walks to the ropes, gestures with both hands at his chest, and pulls out, in mime, his heart, which he throws toward the dim masses.

Tiger Williams spits into the bucket.

Debby squeezes my sweating hand. "When it's all

179

over, Ira, everything, let's move to a little cottage in Vermont or Maine and be farmers." Flashbulbs blind us from all sides. "He said without you, Ira, he would never have had a career. In spite of everything you should be proud."

And you know something, Debby, Jesús—everyone who remembers that night—I am proud. Nobody in that screaming audience, none of the would-be catchers of his heart, is more proud of Jesús than I am. The world has only been with him for a few minutes, but I can feel in my palms the impact of his fists as I caught his jabs over the months of practice. I can see in the international hero the breaker of batteries, holding a sledge-hammer over his shoulder in the Detroit winter. Yes, Jesús, history has carried you past Detroit, past me, and into the beatitude of this moment. But I know as I look at you that you are what I dreamed you would be. True I dreamed it otherwise—less spectacularly—but still I dreamed it while you were in the gym or the junkyard or in the basement watching TV. I always had in my mind the idea of what you might become: Jesús the strong, Jesús the conqueror, Jesús the best of men. What else does champion mean?

The blue-black arms of Tiger Williams cut the air. His power makes a noise, and the sweat flies from his body with each punch.

Suddenly Jesús is disembodied. His feet dance away from some of the blows, but he is clearly somewhere else. His eye is glazed, but in wonder, not in pain. Tiger Williams is a machine, a harvester; Jesús is the gift of nature growing carelessly in the wind and fine weather. The blue-black arms find landing places, but Jesús could care less.

I am up in my seat. "Stop it," I am screaming to his corner, "throw in the towel. Williams will kill him." Salutatti does not look my way. Jesús has not been down yet, but all of the punches are landing now. Williams sets his feet and puts his full weight into each blow. His arms are tired from the constant swinging. "Stop the fight," I am yelling to Salutatti, to Debby, to the backpedaling referee, his white shirt now spotted with the blood of Jesús.

Debby clutches my arm. "He'll be our friend, Ira, when all of it is over. He'll visit us every summer. He'll play with our children. Oh God, don't let them kill him." She sobs against my shoulder. The entire world is up begging Jesús to fall, to stop the onslaught, to go down like a boxer, not stand there like a bloodied martyr.

Williams himself steps back for a moment to gaze at the standing form of his adversary and to catch his breath for another savage flurry. Jesús is like a cloud. He is not stumbling, not faltering, but rolling smoothly across the surface of the ring. His motion is continual. For over sixty seconds he has not even raised his arms in defense. They lie as if paralyzed at his sides, although the legs work as efficiently as ever. The legs are doing a kind of boxer's waltz, circling away from the opposite corner smoothly, automatically, just as he learned to do in Miguel León's instructional film. He is all instinct now. For many seconds he has been out on his feet and I see, suddenly, that he will never fall.

Jesús has trained outside of his body. He is standing now in the realms of pure spirit. He is a block of marble and Tiger Williams some petty Michelangelo chipping away at him. Jesús will fall, but only in geologic time, when the arena withers to sandstone and the great grandchildren of Tiger Williams huddle in the cities of the twenty-second century. I look up at Hoover. He, too, is shaking his head in disbelief. Nobody wants it to go on. The referee looks at Salutatti as if to ask his permission to end it. The Italian sneers and punches the air, his signal for the fight to continue. The contract has called

181

for an end to the technical-knockout rule. The referee can stop the fight only with permission from the manager of the stricken fighter. He, too, is a helpless witness to what now seems Salutatti's plan to execute Jesús on worldwide television.

"It's not Hoover that he's kidnapped, Jesús," I am yelling, "it's you. Go down. Go down and you'll live to fight again and screw girls like Jane Fonda. Oh, Jesús, please." I am sobbing, too, now. Tiger Williams is covered with the blood of Jesús. He has slowed his punches and aims each one as if he is a butcher cutting out a sirloin tip for a demanding customer.

Grandma, what is he proving now? Your shvartzer-Puerto Rican-orphan-communist-assman—what is he proving to anyone, and why is he holding his young life in the air as exposed as your poor bald head against the hospital pillow? The mouthpiece is gone and his teeth are all over the ring. His eyes are closed. His nose is not identifiable in the bloodied recess of his face. I don't know, Bobbe, where it comes from, but for the first time in my life comes the zip of Ira Goldstein. I push Debby aside as if she's a pickpocket. I part the ropes so quickly that they snap like rubber bands. When the referee approaches, my glare alone sends him to a neutral corner. I do not hear the audience. If they're still screaming, their roar is only white noise. I see slowness and silence. Tiger Williams, tired and in tears, points to his piece of work. He spits out his mouthpiece. "The motherfucker won't go down. He wants to git kilt. If I have to, I'll do it." I motion him aside with a nod of my head.

The wet and battered body of Jesús Goldstein I approach. As I come to him I close my own eyes to avoid seeing what two minutes of such ferocity has done to his smiling Latin features. I hug Jesús. The referee tries to part us, but I hug tight and lock my arms around him. "No more, Jesús, no more." My voice is calm. "Dr.

Shimmer will clean you up, my man, and in a few days you'll be good as new."

With his eyes still closed and through his bloody, toothless mouth Jesús' voice comes to me. "Fuck off, Ira," he says. "In the next round I level that coon."

The bell saves me. Cuban police haul me to the back of the arena. From my roost far from ringside, among the noisy rabble, Jesús, I watch as Salutatti orders J. Edgar Hoover's basket lowered into the ring. Yes, the fight is over. Salutatti has admitted the end. The basket comes slowly down, and Hoover in his blue suit and kidskin shoes steps into the blood-stained ring. He shakes the glove of Tiger Williams. The American TV cameras are on these two, but the crowd does not even see them. For in the middle of the ring, Jesús has entered the basket of Hoover's captivity and now, blinded and beaten as he is, Jesús is being raised aloft. Slowly, like the flag, he ascends. He raises his arms now to throw bloodied kisses. Debby has pushed her way to my side at the rear of the arena. The policemen forget me in the spectacle. She takes my hand and leads me out of the auditorium.

"I wanted to save him."

"I know," she says, "you did your best." She pulls me toward Vermont. When I look back for one last glimpse of Jesús, he is nearing the rafters, ascending still.

183